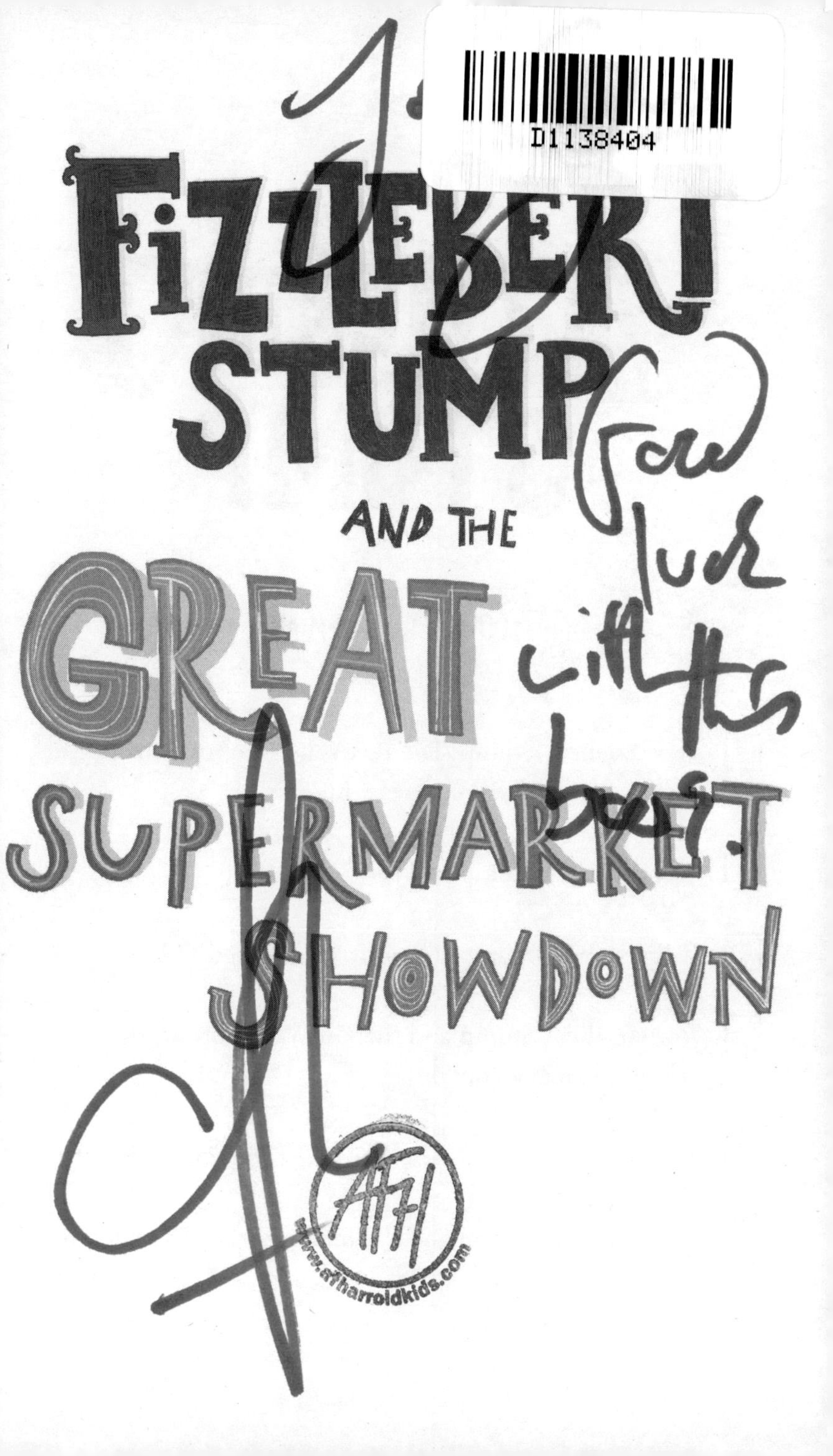
D1138404
FIZZLEBERT
STUMP
AND THE
GREAT
SUPERMARKET
SHOWDOWN
AFH
www.afharroldkids.com

FIZZLEBERT STUMP

DO YOU HAVE THEM ALL?

- ☐ 1 Fizzlebert Stump: The Boy Who Ran Away from the Circus and Joined the Library
- ☐ 2 Fizzlebert Stump and the Bearded Boy
- ☐ 3 Fizzlebert Stump: The Boy Who Cried Fish
- ☐ 4 Fizzlebert Stump and the Girl Who Lifted Quite Heavy Things
- ☐ 5 Fizzlebert Stump: The Boy Who Did P.E. in His Pants
- ☐ 6 Fizzlebert Stump and the Supermarket Showdown

READERS SAY ...

'It's funny, fantastic and ridiculous. I would put it in my top five books of all time, and I've read a lot of books – probably at least three thousand'

Milo, age 8

'Evil old people, a sea lion in a sparkly jacket and a lion called Charles with false teeth! What more could you want? I laughed my socks off'

Florence, age 9

'This book is like the 100 best books in the world put together!'

Hugo, age 10

'A great story that made me fizz with laughter!'

Felix, age 12

Also by A.F. Harrold

The FIZZLEBERT STUMP series

Illustrated by Sarah Horne

Fizzlebert Stump: The Boy Who Ran Away from the Circus and Joined the Library

Fizzlebert Stump and the Bearded Boy

Fizzlebert Stump: The Boy Who Cried Fish

Fizzlebert Stump and the Girl Who Lifted Quite Heavy Things

Fizzlebert Stump: the Boy Who Did P.E. in His Pants

Fizzlebert Stump and the Supermarket Showdown

Illustrated by Joe Todd-Stanton

Greta Zargo and the Death Robots from Outer Space

Greta Zargo and the Amoeba Monsters from the Middle of the Earth

The Imaginary

The Afterwards

Illustrated by Emily Gravett

The Song from Somewhere Else

Illustrated by Levi Pinfold

FIZZLEBERT STUMP

AND THE GREAT SUPERMARKET SHOWDOWN

A.F. HARROLD

ILLUSTRATED BY Sarah Horne

BLOOMSBURY
CHILDREN'S BOOKS
LONDON OXFORD NEW YORK NEW DELHI SYDNEY

BLOOMSBURY CHILDREN'S BOOKS
Bloomsbury Publishing Plc
50 Bedford Square, London WC1B 3DP, UK
29 Earlsfort Terrace, Dublin 2, Ireland

BLOOMSBURY, BLOOMSBURY CHILDREN'S BOOKS and the Diana
logo are trademarks of Bloomsbury Publishing Plc

First published in Great Britain in 2015 by Bloomsbury Publishing Plc
This edition published in Great Britain in 2021 by Bloomsbury Publishing Plc

A catalogue record for this book is available from the British Library

ISBN: PB: 978-1-5266-1648-7; eBook: 978-1-4088-6946-8

2 4 6 8 10 9 7 5 3 1

Typeset in Great Britain by Hewer Text UK Ltd, Edinburgh
Printed and bound in Great Britain by CPI Group (UK) Ltd, Croydon CR0 4YY

FOR KATE PAICE, WITHOUT WHOM ...

CHAPTER FOUR

In which a boy carries some bags and into which some rain falls

Fizzlebert Stump sighed wearily under the weight of the great weights he sighed wearily under the weight of. Each of his two small hands held the straining handle of a bulging bag filled with frozen chickens and cans of soup and heads of broccoli and bottles of fizzy pop (among other things). The plastic was stretching, becoming sharp and thin, and was cutting off the blood supply to his fingers which were growing numb. They were turning white, and heading towards a shade of blue that fingers weren't ever intended to be.

He heaved and –

Hang on …

I've not done the introductions yet, have I?

Here we are at the very beginning of the book and I've just plunged straight in without even saying, 'Hello,' and without explaining what's going on or what the plan is.

Sorry about that.

My mistake.

Let me start again …

Hello, I'm the author of this book. I'm the person who's going to be talking to you, inside your head, through your eyes, for the next two hundred and eighty-seven pages. (Unless, of course, you throw the book away right now (and who could blame you after I messed the beginning up so royally?).)

This isn't the first book I've written about Fizzlebert Stump and his various 'mildly amusing adventures' (*The Lascaux Echo*), but perhaps it's the first one *you've* read, so for the sake of any new readers I'd best start with a few Key Facts:

(1) Fizzlebert Stump is a boy who lives in a travelling circus.

(2) A travelling circus is a circus that goes from place to place.

(3) A plaice is a sort of fish.

(4) Fish is one of Fizz's friends in the circus.

(5) Fish is a sea lion.

(6) Fish likes fish.

(7) A plaice is an example of a sort of fish that Fish likes.

(8) Once upon a time Fizz (which is what

we call Fizzlebert Stump most of the time in order to save on ink, because we're environmentally minded like that) put his head inside a lion's mouth (and took it out again) to wow the audiences, but nowadays (since the lion retired) he does a strong-man act with his father, Mr Stump.
(9) Mr Stump, Fizz's dad, is a strongman.
(10) Mrs Stump, Fizz's mum, is a clown. When she's got her make-up on she's called The Fumbling Gloriosus, but when she doesn't she's just called Gloria.

'Aha!' you might be saying to yourself, waving your finger in the air as if you've just had a brilliant idea. 'The reason Fizz was sighing under the weight of the heavy bags mentioned by accident at the very beginning is because he's practising for the strongman act. It's obvious!'

'Well,' I'd say back to you, 'you're wrong. You couldn't be more wronger.'

'Aha!' you might say. 'There's no such word as "wronger".'

To which I'd reply, 'You couldn't be more wrongerer about that, but we're not here to discuss vocabulary, so let's get on with the story.'

Fizzlebert Stump sighed wearily under the weight of the great weights he sighed wearily under the weight of. Each of his two small hands held a straining handle of a bulging bag filled with frozen peas and cans of rice pudding and bundles of carrots and bottles of orange squash (among other things). The plastic was stretching, becoming sharp and thin, and was cutting off the blood supply to his fingers which were becoming numb. They were turning white, and heading towards a shade of blue that fingers weren't ever intended to be.

He heaved and hefted the bags into the open boot of the old lady's car.

'Good,' she said, as Fizz rubbed life back into his stinging hands.

She climbed into the car and drove away, leaving him stood in the middle of the car park.

It was beginning to rain.

Fizz's uniform itched.

His hands hurt.

He sighed, deeply.

'Stump!' a voice shouted from somewhere

over in the direction of that big white building you hadn't noticed because I hadn't mentioned it yet. 'Stop dawdling! Get back here! Now!'

Still rubbing his fingers Fizz trudged grudgingly back across the car park, avoiding the cars (most of which were parked, but one or two of which were moving), and grumbling grumpily to himself.

'How did it ever come to this?' he asked.

The world answered him with a distant rumble of thunder and a dribble of raindrops down the back of his neck, which wasn't really much of an answer, if you think about it.

As he reached the big white building I mentioned earlier he was met by a short, pointy-faced man with a clipboard, a pen, a frown, two sideburns and a gaggle of elderly women hanging round him.

'You need to be faster, Stump. Mrs Jones here's been waiting five minutes. She's in parking space ninety-seven. These six bags.'

He pointed at six bags of shopping sat neatly at the feet of a particularly unpleasant-looking old lady.

She smiled toothlessly at the man with the clipboard and said, 'Fank you, darlin'.'

'Get on with it, Stump.'

Parking space ninety-seven was right over the other side of the car park. Fizz looked at the six bags. It wasn't that they were too heavy for him, but the plastic they were made from was so cheap he was afraid his fingers would sooner or later be chopped off, or that

it would break and spill the old lady's shopping all over the tarmac, and that would be almost as bad.

'Shall I use one of the trolleys?' he asked.

Even the rain fell silent.

The old ladies looked at the man with the clipboard.

The man with the clipboard's clipboard twitched.

'A trolley?' the man with the clipboard said. 'A,' he really dragged out the pause, 'trolley?'

He was doing that thing that people with clipboards often do, which was shouting, but really quietly. He was angry, that was clear from the fact that his face had just turned red, and he said the two words ('a' and 'trolley') with a smear of venom and unpleasantness that made the quietness of his voice *feel* like a force ten gale.

But then, all of a sudden, he smiled, the rain splashed and the old ladies rippled a little laughter out of their tiny tight mouths as he said, 'But, Stump, it's raining. I can't risk the trolleys getting rusty. That's why we've got you.'

There was nothing for it. Fizz shifted uncomfortably in the scratchy supermarket uniform, slipped his hands into the handle-holes of the plastic bags, and, three on each side, began walking towards parking space ninety-seven.

'Stop! Stop!' shouted the man with the clipboard.

Fizz stopped.

'Oi! Mr Surprise!' the man with the

clipboard shouted. 'Umbrella for Mrs Liver-smell. Quick! Quick!'

Fizz heard the old lady say, 'Oh, darlin', yer too kind.'

'It's nothing,' the man with the clipboard said, oilily.

Fizz trudged off through the rain, droplets dribbling down his nose, the thin plastic cutting into his fingers, as an old woman hobbled along at his side, smelling of lavender and newt, with the tall figure of Dr Surprise walking beside her, holding an umbrella over her head.

Dr Surprise was dressed, like Fizz, in a supermarket uniform.

He stared straight ahead, as if hypnotised. Except he wasn't hypnotised because he was unhypnotisable, being the circus's hypnotist (and magician, mind reader and illusionist). He was just miserable, itchy and cold.

He edged the umbrella over to one side so that half of it was covering Fizz as well as Mrs Liversmell.

'Surprise!' yelled the clipboarded gentleman. 'Umbrellas are for customers' use only!'

'Sorry, Fizz,' the doctor said, shifting it back over the old lady.

They trudged, at the pace of an old woman, across the car park.

Now, even the newest readers of this book, the ones who've never met Fizz before, and who only know what I told you in the list of Key Facts a little earlier, will be saying to themselves, 'What the juggling gerbil's going on here? You told me this was a book about a circus and all we've got is some nonsense about customer service in a supermarket car park. This isn't what I expected a Fizzlebert Stump book to be about. Where do I get my money back?'

Well, let me say just two things.

Firstly: be patient and everything will make sense and be explained and so on, soon.

And secondly: refunds are nothing to do with me.

(If you *really* want your money back you'll need to take the book back to where you bought it, with the receipt, and it'll need to be looking as good as new. Were your hands clean? Did you drop it in the bath? Or in the mud? I hope not, for your sake.)

* * *

For the rest of us, the story will continue in the next chapter. In fact, we'll be going back in time in order to understand what just happened. OK, so hang on tight for Chapter One.

CHAPTER ONE

In which a man makes an announcement and in which a boy does not have a haddock in his pocket

I am taking you back half an hour to before the rain and then back slightly further (another three weeks, two days and four hours) to the fateful morning when the Ringmaster summoned the whole circus together in the Mess Tent.

Breakfast was over.

Cook was grumbling because there was washing-up to do.

Fizz, and his mum and dad (who had had breakfast in their caravan (toffee apple surprise (the surprise being it had actually been cornflakes and jam))), strolled in and sat on a bench at the back, not expecting anything untoward to be about to unfold.

It was quite normal for the Ringmaster to call everyone together now and then. It's the easiest way to share news. (At school you have assembly, at work people have staff meetings, in the middle of a lake you have six thousand flamingos. It's the same thing, really.)

But then the Ringmaster spoke and everything went weird.

Clowns held their breaths.

Captain Fox-Dingle, the animal trainer, held his breath.

Mary and Maureen Twitchery, the acrobatic sisters, held their breaths.

Don Pedro Alfonso Zaragoza de Manchester-Sur-le-Mer, the famous botanist, apologised and left, since he wasn't a member of the circus and had merely wandered into the Mess Tent on the trail of a type of grass that looked almost different to all other types of grass, but not quite. Still, he held his breath as he did so.

'My friends,' the Ringmaster began. 'My many friends. My many good friends. My good many friends. I have news, and there's no easy way to tell you the news that I have to tell you. What I could do is make a joke and play the ukulele and sing a little song about why custard is yellow and why birds are feathery, but that would just be me dodging the difficult matter of my telling you the news.'

There was some uncomfortable murmuring at the possibility of the Ringmaster singing, but as soon as he didn't people relaxed.

'I've sold the circus,' he said.

People stopped relaxing.

(A stilt-walker stopped relaxing so suddenly he fell off his stilts and landed on one of Apology Cheesemutter's 'mice' (which were actually dogs dressed as mice, although no one ever mentioned this). Fortunately it was only a small stilt-walker and quite a large 'mouse' so there were no injuries, although the barking did drown out the Ringmaster's explanation.)

He began again.

'Calm down, everyone,' he said, in his most authoritatively Ringmasterish tone. 'It's not as bad as it sounds. We're still a circus, it's just we're a circus now that belongs to Pinkbottle's Supermarket. Think of it as … sponsorship.'

'Um, Ringmaster,' asked Miss Tremble, the woman who trained a dozen white horses with feathery headdresses to parade around in circles doing marvellous trotting tricks while she rode on their backs in a sequined costume doing tricks and turns and tumbles of her own, 'why have you sold the circus? Were we … in trouble?'

'Well,' the Ringmaster began, and stopped.

He took his top hat off and dusted the top with his sleeve.

'Um,' he said, starting but not going on.

He put his top hat back on his head and dusted his sleeve with his hand.

'Any other questions?' he asked.

Bongo Bongoton, the circus's finest mime, made some movements with his hands and body, while a saddish look crossed his face.

('What's the most miserable vegetable in the world?' asked Unnecessary Sid.

When no one replied he pointed at Bongo's face and said, 'A saddish.')

'Now, that's not fair, Bongo,' the Ringmaster said, watching the mime's mime and blushing red. 'I have been promised by Mr Pinkbottle himself that there will be no top down reorganisation of the circus. I expect we'll probably just have to wear Pinkbottle Supermarket badges on our costumes and print Pinkbottle Supermarket adverts in our programmes. For the rest of it, it'll be the same. You'll still get paid every week.'

Naturally this set everyone's minds at ease. Who could you trust if not your Ringmaster? A Ringmaster is to a circus what Father Christmas is to North Pole Elves: he or she is the person in charge who can be trusted to make the right decisions while you just get on with doing your job (making toys or doing backflips).

Every week the Ringmaster gives you a little envelope with your wages in, carefully counted out and countersigned by Barry Numbers (the circus accountant who won a surprise holiday to Acapulco a fortnight before this chapter began in a competition he didn't remember entering) and you put some of it in your bottom drawer (for savings) and a little in your pocket for pocket money and you were happy thinking about lifting up heavy things or dodging custard or dressing your horses up with feathery headdresses (and so on).

So, as you can imagine, hearing that the new circus owner, Mr Pinkbottle of Pinkbottle's Supermarket fame, would continue to pay them as normal made the Ringmaster's worrying announcement seem less worrying. People breathed easily and went about the rest of their day rehearsing their acts as if it were a normal Tuesday.

But it wasn't a normal Tuesday.

It was Monday.

(Now, I know we've not had very much Fizzlebert Stump in this chapter so far, but he was there, at the back with his mum and dad, who held their breaths and then let them go again along with everyone else. The reason I've not paid much attention to him is because what the Ringmaster was saying was more important than knowing that Fizz was mostly just being nose-nudged by Fish, the circus sea

lion, who refused to believe that the boy didn't have a haddock in his pocket.)

OK, now I've shown you that scene, I ought to let you know that nothing else very interesting happened that day. After that evening's show the circus packed itself away and trundled through the night to the next town they were due to visit and it was there, the following morning that the next chapter happened.

CHAPTER TWO

In which a boy overhears a plot and in which contracts are discussed

Fizzlebert Stump unbuckled himself from his bed and sat up.

Outside he could hear birds singing and the sound of folk at work. (These were the riggers, who put the Big Top up and tie the guy ropes down and all that sort of physical stuff.) Somewhere in the distance he could hear Captain Fox-Dingle doing his exercises and Dr Surprise plucking fresh clover for Flopples (his rabbit).

(It can be hard to hear clover plucking, but fortunately Dr Surprise gave a little cry every time he found a good bit and shrilly shouted, 'Oh! Clover! Clover! Lovely leafy little clover!' which helped.)

The sun was shining through the curtains and it looked like it was a beautiful day.

Fizz loved waking up in a new town because it was like starting reading a new book: you never quite knew what you were in for, although it was probably going to be pretty good since you're a circus strongboy living, as they say, the dream.

'Breakfast, Fizz,' his mum said, putting a plate on the table in front of him.

Fizz yawned, stretched and lifted his spoon.

'Thanks, Mum,' he said, looking down at his bowl of Spam cake and bran flake. (The clown-ish part of her brain insisted that rhyming foods were funny, even when she didn't have her make-up on. Fizz had eaten some odd combinations in his time, but this one was new.)

'It's good for you,' his dad said, sensing Fizz's culinary caution. 'The Spam builds muscles and the bran keeps you –'

There was a banging at their door and a voice shouted from outside, 'Meeting in the Mess Tent! Ten minutes!'

'Two days in a row?' Mrs Stump said. 'That's not normal.'

Normal or not, it was happening.

Another meeting!

Dun-duh-daaahhh! (See, it's an exciting book this one, with music in.)

Still it was ten minutes away, so Fizz had time to tuck into his Spam cake and bran-flake breakfast, which wasn't as bad as he'd imagined it might be. (He didn't find the bran-flake until the last spoonful, which helped.)

As the Stumps trudged across to the Mess Tent they bumped into Dr Surprise.

'Ah!' he shouted in shock, since he'd been looking the other way.

'Dr Surprise,' Fizz said. 'How is Flopples this morning?'

'Oh, Fizzlebert,' the doctor said. 'What with this meeting being sprung on us unexpectedly I've not had time to get back to the caravan to give her her breakfast.'

A wilting bunch of clover drooped in his hand.

'I'll take it, if you like?' Fizz offered.

(Although he was a member of the circus as much as the next person, he was also a boy and did find that meetings sometimes got a bit dull. He fidgeted and sometimes snored. It wouldn't matter if he missed the beginning of this one, would it?)

'Would you?' Dr Surprise asked. 'She likes you, you know. This'll put you right up in her good books. But make sure she doesn't gobble. Just a nibble at a time. Yes?'

'Is that OK, Mum?' Fizz asked.

'If you're quick,' his mum said. 'Then straight to the Mess Tent.'

'Of course,' Fizz said.

He left the grown-ups and ran between wagons and past vehicles to Dr Surprise's caravan, a beautiful silver house on wheels with his name painted on the side.

Fizz mounted the steps and opened the door.

'Flopples,' he called. 'Are you here?'

There was a snuffling noise from inside Dr Surprise's spare hat which was sat on the fold-down kitchen table.

Fizz peered down at the rabbit, who looked up at him as if to say, 'Where's my breakfast?'

'Here's your clover,' Fizz said, lowering a few leaves into the hat.

Flopples snatched them, those great yellow-white teeth flashing scarily close to his fingers. But Fizz didn't flinch. He wasn't afraid of a rabbit, not when he'd faced crocodiles and saboteurs and headless ghosts and evil old people and Independent Truant Officers and bullies and swarms of clockwork locusts and a sad dolphin called Clive (important note:

some, though not all, of these encounters happen in the other *Fizzlebert Stump* books).

He bravely lowered another sprig of clover towards Flopples's snapping, snatching jaws, and as he did so he heard someone say something.

'I hate circuses,' said a voice from just outside the caravan. (It sounded like a woman.) 'They give me the shivers.'

'Well then,' said a second voice (a man's voice, Fizz thought), 'you're going to love what happens next.'

'I think it's the sequins and the leotards,' said the first voice. 'I find them a bit weird. I mean, what sort of sensible person wears sequins? It can't be safe.'

'No more sequins,' said the second voice. 'That's a promise.'

Uh-oh, thought Fizz.

He didn't recognise either of the voices, but he recognised the gist of what they were saying. They were saying that *something was going to happen to the circus.* (And it wasn't going to be a good thing. Not if there wouldn't be sequins.)

Fizz had dealt with people who wanted to put an end to his circus before. None of them had outwitted him, not in the end, but he knew that this first bit was always tricky. He couldn't just run up to the Ringmaster and say, 'I heard someone say they were going to ruin the circus,' because the Ringmaster wouldn't believe him. That was grown-ups for you, they never believed you, not until it was all over and the villains were tied up and confessing.

What Fizz needed was *evidence*.

He dropped the last of the clover into the hat, picked a small grey metal thing up off the side and tiptoed over to the caravan window. (He had to climb up and perch on the edge of the sink to reach it, but that was easy enough.)

He parted the net curtain a couple of centimetres and peered out.

In the alley between Dr Surprise's caravan and the next one over (an orange campervan owned by Fred and Kurt Berkson, The Tattooed Triplets (Sam, their brother, had left the circus years earlier to become an abacus salesman)) were two people.

One was a short man with big sideburns and a white suit.

The other was a tall woman with no sideburns and a nervous expression.

It was probably she who distrusted sequins.

He willed them to say more. To outline their plan and to do so clearly and loudly.

He lifted the small grey metal thing he'd picked up and pressed the button labelled *record*.

(Dr Surprise used this little tape recorder to jot down ideas for tricks and illusions when they came to him. He sometimes stopped in the middle of the history lessons he gave Fizz to click the red button and say something like, 'Item: flags of all nations, but with breeds of dog?')

The woman in the alley said, 'Do you promise, Mr P? No more sequins?'

'When have I ever told you a lie?' the man replied. 'This time tomorrow there won't be no circus no more. They'll all be in uniform and stacking shelves for me. This was the best five hundred quid I ever spent.'

'That's a lot of money for a few pictures, Mr P.'

'Yeah, but look where they've got us. This ex-circus is all mine now. Mine, I tell you!'

Then he laughed the sort-of laugh and it sounded like the sort of laugh a villain in a black and white film would laugh, possibly while twirling a moustache.

Except … the man had *no moustache*.

Fizz's brain was whirling.

Mr P?

Was this Mr Pinkbottle, the supermarket man? What did he mean: they'd all be stacking shelves? In uniform? No circus no more? What? *What?* WHAT!?

Fizz panicked. The Ringmaster had been fooled into doing something *rash*, something *wrong*! Fizz had to save the day. He had the evidence, now all he had to do was run and find the Ringmaster and play him the tape and then they could cancel the deal, give Mr Pinkbottle back whatever he'd paid for the circus and things could simply get back to normal.

He pressed *stop* on the tape recorder and reached out backwards with his foot to find the ground.

As he did so, not being an expert acrobat, he slipped, stumbled, fell and, despite his circus training in safe-falling, banged his head on either the floor or the way down.

The caravan went black.

Fizz woke up and opened his eyes.

It was dark.

And furry.

Had he knocked himself out and been asleep so long that night had fallen?

If that was the case, why had no one found him?

And why was the night furry?

He went to rub his eyes and found there was a black top hat in the way.

Underneath the hat was a dozing rabbit, which he pushed off his face quickly, with an apology.

It all came flooding back.

'Sorry, Flopples,' he said, climbing to his feet, 'I've got to go warn the Ringmaster. I've got to find my mum and dad. We're all in great danger!'

He glanced at the clock on the wall.

He'd only been unconscious for ten minutes, maybe even less. He still had time.

With the tape recorder in his hand he ran out of the caravan and wound his way through the circus to the Mess Tent.

It was lucky the Ringmaster had called a

second meeting, Fizz told himself, because it meant that everyone would be in the same place at the same time and that made his raising the alarm about the devious supermarketeers threatening their circus that much easier.

Almost out of breath and with a sea lion flolloping behind him (in Fish's brain the sight of a running boy meant: *fish?*) Fizz burst through the Mess Tent's flapway and pushed his way through the assembled crowd shouting, 'Ringmaster! Ringmaster! Pinkbottle's not interested in the circus, he wants us to wear uniforms and work for him. Super*market*! Not Super *circus*!'

He stopped shouting when he realised he had reached the front. Also when he realised everyone was staring at him. Also when he

realised the Ringmaster was stood beside the two people he'd overheard scheming their plans. Also when he realised he'd obviously interrupted something.

'Fizzlebert Stump,' the Ringmaster said. 'What's wrong with you? You burst in here shouting your lungs out when Mr Pinkbottle is speaking … I've never known you to be so rude before.'

'But,' Fizz sputtered, 'he's going to stop the circus being a circus!'

'We know, Fizz,' his dad said, stepping out of the crowd and putting a hand on his son's shoulder. 'That's what we've been talking about for the last ten minutes.'

'Oh,' said Fizz.

That had rather ruined his surprise. They already knew. And they were already discussing it.

'Oh,' he said again.

Fortunately he was saved from being any more embarrassed as Fish, like a guided fish-seeking missile homing in on a non-existent fish, came bursting into the Mess Tent, knocking circus performers over like skittles and landing on top of Fizz with a great mackerel-flavoured belch that ruffled the Ringmaster's hair and soured the atmosphere.

'Maybe we should take a break?' Mr Pinkbottle said, riffling a wad of papers in his hand and peering down at Fizzlebert. 'Everyone back here in fifteen minutes. Yes?'

The tent emptied out, with grumbling and foot shuffling. Even from underneath a sea lion, and with his nose full of coconut matting, Fizz could tell the atmosphere had been unhappy before Fish had added his aromas to it.

'Come on, Fizz,' his dad said, lifting the wriggling Fish from off his back. 'Let's go get some fresh air.'

'Actually,' said Mr Pinkbottle, 'I'd like to have a word with you three.'

Fizz clambered to his feet and looked around at his mum and dad.

'What do you want?' his mum said, not in a jolly clowny way, but in a jolly frowny way. (She didn't have her make-up on and was, therefore, being serious.)

'You three are Stumps, yes?'

They nodded.

'I have been looking through these contracts,' Mr Pinkbottle said, waving the pile of papers in his hand.

Fizz didn't remember signing any contract. He hadn't *joined* the circus, he'd been born into it. His mum and dad were already there when he was born and they'd just stayed.

Mr Pinkbottle looked him straight in the eye.

'Your parents,' he said, not in the most pleasant tone of voice, hardly sounding friendly or kind or warm or welcoming or charitable at all, 'signed good old-fashioned British Board of Circuses' Classic Twenty-One-Year Tour-of-Duty Contracts. As you know these contracts are watertight, unbreakable and have eleven more years to run. So it looks like we're stuck together.'

'Oh,' said Mr Stump. 'I knew we should have –'

Let me, your author, interrupt here for a moment …

Look, *I* know and *you* know that discussing contracts is boring and this is supposed to be an exciting and funny novel telling you about the zany adventures Fizz has in his crazy circus life, but it's important, just quickly, that these contracts get discussed.

So, instead of listening to the conversation the Stumps are having with Mr Pinkbottle, which has a lot of this way and that way, back and forth, arguing and discussing, I'll give you a quick rundown of what's going on. OK?

Most people in Mr Pinkbottle's brave new circus are being 'let go' (which really means 'asked to leave' or 'sacked' or 'fired'). The supermarket man has no use for them and is waving them goodbye.

Some people though, including the Stumps, have signed special contracts that mean they can't be sacked. With a British Board of Circuses' Classic Twenty-One-Year Tour-of-Duty Contract they were always guaranteed work, but also they couldn't resign. (Or rather they *could*, but when it was printed in the BBC Newsletter that they'd reneged on a BBC contract they'd never be invited to sign another contract with a circus again, classic or not.)

And it didn't matter whether your contract was owned by a Ringmaster or a Supermarket-master, a contract is a contract and simply says (the BBC keep their wording simple) 'do the work' (if they printed a different contract for each different act saying 'juggle three balls at the same time' or 'teach fleas to sing popular tunes from Gilbert and Sullivan operettas' or 'pour custard down your trousers', it would take ages). So that was what the Stumps had to do: the work Mr Pinkbottle told them to do, since he was the one who owned the contracts now.

Now, back to the Mess Tent . . .

'You belong to me now!' the be-sideburned supermarketeer shouted, ending the argument.

As he did so, Fish, the sea lion who'd been nosing through the breakfast washing-up and whose whiskers were dripping with very un-fishy porridge, was lifted up by six burly men with fluffy white walrus moustaches and little hats with anchors on the front.

Fish struggled, but they held him firm and hauled him out of the Mess Tent.

'Stop! Come back! Put that sea lion down!' Fizz shouted, running after them.

'Stump!' shouted Mr Pinkbottle. 'Get back here!'

Fizz turned on his heel in the flapway.

'But they're Fish-napping … I mean sea lion-napping Fish! We've got to –'

'They're doing nothing of the sort,' Mr Pinkbottle's companion said, making notes on her clipboard. 'That animal now belongs to Old Hempleford Aquarium. Those men have come to take him away.'

'Um,' said the Ringmaster, interrupting with a tiny cough. 'I really must put my foot down, Mr Pinkbottle. Breaking the circus up and selling our friends off to various zoos and aquaria was never part of the deal.'

Mr Pinkbottle looked the Ringmaster up and down (mainly 'up', being a head shorter than him) with a pitiless eye, and said, 'I have altered the deal, *Your Highness*. Pray I don't alter it any further.'

The Ringmaster blushed and gabbled but, really, that was all there was to it. Nothing he said made any difference, and if the Ringmaster couldn't change the man's mind what chance did Fizz have?

He pushed past the woman with the clip-board and ran outside.

All around him the circus was fading away.

The Big Top, which had been half put up, had been half taken down (the half that had been put up, of course, not the other half (which would have also needed putting up before they could take it down (and after that they'd still have the other half (the first half) to take down too, which would've all been rather a lot of effort))).

Some caravans had already been hauled away, by acts who had been sacked, leaving gaps in the circus-town.

There was a woman wrapping sticky tape around the snout of Kate the crocodile. Captain Fox-Dingle stood idly by, his tiny toothbrush moustache twitching on his top lip. Kate had been sold, like Fish had. (Fizz didn't know who had bought the crocodile, but I can tell you it was Duck'n'Gooseland, a duck and goose-themed wildlife park just outside West Qualmsworth whose owner wanted to add some excitement to the place.)

No one was rehearsing.

Even the clowns were just stood around, in a gaggle, without falling over or saying anything stupid. One of them, Dick Turnip, was eating custard (a great clown comfort food) from a bowl *without spilling a drop*.

Fizz had never seen the circus so depressed. After all it had been through, after all the things he'd saved it from, it was ending like this. Not with a bang, but a shrug.

His mum and dad walked with him back to their caravan and awaited instructions.

* * *

I think there are two good ways to end chapters. One is to stop in the middle of something really exciting or dangerous so that the reader goes, 'Oh! Golly! I've got to find out what happens next!' and then turns the page eagerly, breathlessly and without hesitation or having dinner.

The other way is to just let a fog of gloominess and defeat linger like an unpleasant smell, in the hope that the reader will think, 'Well, maybe something more interesting will happen in the next bit.'

Can you tell what sort of ending this chapter has?

CHAPTER THREE

In which something more interesting happens and in which punishments are dealt out

The next morning Fizz woke up early.

There was a banging on the outside of the caravan.

It was what had woken him up.

Bang! Bang! Bang!

It was still dark. It was that early.

Bang! Bang! Bang!

He struggled out of bed in the gloom

and bumped into his mum and dad, who were also miserably bumping around in the caravan.

'No time for home breakfast today, Fizz,' his dad said. 'We've got to report to Mr Pinkbottle. You'd best get dressed.'

The day before they'd driven their caravan out of the park where they'd been parked and into the small private 'deliveries only' car park at the back of Pinkbottle's Supermarket.

It hadn't just been Fizz and his mum and dad, there were a handful of other acts who had also been retained by the new regime. Most people had been let go and had gone. It had been sad to see so many friends thinking about what to put in their 'Act In Need of a Circus' advert in the next issue of the British

Board of Circuses' Newsletter.

Fizz and the other remaining ex-circus acts had been given plastic bags containing supermarket uniforms and told to be ready for six the next morning.

In a circus, as in much of showbusiness (a world of late nights and bright lights), six o'clock in the morning is a near-mythical time of day, heard about, whispered of, but rarely encountered. Certainly it wasn't a time Fizz remembered ever meeting.

As he climbed out of the caravan, itching in his ill-fitting uniform, he looked around and saw that no one else was having a happy meeting with the time either. They were all looking about themselves, bleary-eyed, yawning, still in shock from their sudden change of circumstance.

Besides the three Stumps there was Dr Surprise, Percy Late (of Percy Late and his Spinning Plate fame), Emerald Sparkles (the knife thrower) and Mr Sparkles (her fifth husband), Captain Fox-Dingle, William Edgebottom (who, when made up and in costume was Bongo Bongoton, the mime) and Madame Plume de Matant (the 'French' fortune teller) and the Ringmaster himself.

They all looked stupid and unimpressive in their stripy supermarket uniforms. There wasn't a single sequin, feather or bright colour to be seen. And even though they were in uniforms and uniforms are meant to make you look smart, these didn't. They weren't very well ironed and it seemed they'd all been given uniforms of more or less the same size, which meant that Fizz's

was too big (even with the sleeves and trouser legs rolled up) and his dad's was too small.

'All right, you horrible lot,' Mr Pinkbottle shouted, as if he'd just woken up from a dream in which he'd been a sergeant major, and wanted to try it out in real life.

He was stood on the steps at the back of the supermarket and with him was the woman with the clipboard (whose name, they discovered at some point not interesting enough to have its own paragraph, was Mrs Leavings).

It seemed supermarket owners and their clipboard-wielding assistants didn't have to wear uniforms. They both had on smart suits, crisply ironed and sort of, but not quite, expensive-looking.

'This is your first day doing *real* work. But I believe you have the capabilities to do what you are told and to do it well. I believe in you. And so, as a display of my faith in your abilities, I want you to know that, because I'm kind and trusting, I shall be making *no allowances at all*. Any *breakages*, any *delays*, any *complaints* from the wretched scum who soil my floors with their dirty shoes to buy themselves little treats or to do the family shop ...' He paused to wipe a speckle of spittle from his spittle-speckled chin. 'Anything goes wrong and your pay will be docked and you'll be sent to work in the cold store, with no gloves.'

Long and unnecessary digression warning! Feel free to skip ahead.

Now, I don't know if you've ever had a real job. I mean, the sort of thing where you have to get up in the morning, every day, and go off somewhere and do what you're told by someone who thinks they're better than you, just because they've been there longer or have a fancy clipboard.

It's been a very long time since I had a proper job, and I can hardly remember what it was like having to get up every morning, early. (Which isn't to say I don't get up every morning, because I do. This writing lark isn't something you can just do in the afternoons. Oh no. I'm writing this paragraph at nine minutes past ten on a Tuesday morning, for example, which gives you an idea of how dedicated I am to making these books for you.)

The point is, I don't have a foreman or a manager stood in the doorway of my study tapping their watch or looking over my shoudler, tutting and saying, 'Well, Harrold, you've spelt "shoulder" wrong again, you flipping idiot. If you don't concentrate I'll flipping well get someone in here who *can* spell. You're not the only one writing books, you know. Writers like you are ten a penny, they're queuing up outside. You'd better buck your ideas up, mister.'

And, to be honest, I'm very glad I don't have a manager like that. (I do have an editor, called Zöe, who looks at the words in the book when I send them to her and she's very nice and appreciates me for the unique talent I am and feeds me tea and biscuits when I go to London to visit her. She wouldn't mind if

I spelt shoulder shoudler because she understands that the odd shoudler isn't the end of the world and we can easily change it before we sell the book to you or your parents.)

Fizz and his circus chums, however, didn't have the good fortune of being employed by someone as kind as Zöe. They had a right monster peering over their shoulders. Oh, it wasn't good. As you'll see.

Long and unnecessary digression ends here! Feel free to continue reading.

On that first day Madame Plume de Matant was set to work on the cheese counter. Perhaps it was because she was (sort of) French and a lot of very fine cheese is French too (such as *le Cheddar* and *le Double Gloucester*).

Had Mr Pinkbottle known Madame Plume de Matant longer he would have known that not only was she fraudulently French and lactose intolerant, but that she was also *very* fond of cheese. The last two facts didn't make for the most comfortable of mornings.

Every time a customer came by and said, 'Could I have two hundred grams of *le Edam*, please?' Madame Plume de Matant couldn't resist cutting a little sliver for herself, and gobbling it while wrapping the customer's portion. By the time she said, 'Is that all?' she could already feel the gurgling and bubbling beginning inside her stomach.

By mid-morning tea breaktime she *knew* she shouldn't eat any more cheese. In fact she knew she shouldn't have eaten *any* cheese at all, but sometimes … what can you do?

When she came back from her break she found a few more little chunks and offcuts of cheese accidentally making their way past her lips.

'Ooh la la,' she murmured as the ripe taste of some creamy mature mouldy gooey *le Stilton* danced around her mouth.

A moment later it was, 'Oh dearie me,' as her stomach began rebelling, bubbling acidly and turning itself over and over like a pillow in the night, unable to find the comfortable cool side.

Food intolerances manifest themselves in different ways in different people. For some it's repeated urgent visits to the loo, for others it's sickly acidic burping. For Madame Plume de Matant it was wind, or as she would say, if she had known the French term: '*le vent*'.

By lunchtime she had, shall we say, *ventilated* the whole of the cheese counter with a perfume created by the combination of the lactose in the cheese and the army of bacteria that inhabited her insides (they're inside you too). It wasn't exactly Chanel No. 5. It was cheesy, but cheesy with a faint undertone of compost. Cheesy with a hint of onion at the edge. Cheesy with a sledgehammer of *Keep Away!* behind the cheesiness.

People kept away.

A dog fainted.

Mr Pinkbottle was as good as his word (or 'as bad as his word', perhaps) and after lunch (and after all the windows had been opened and Dr Surprise had been instructed to wander around wafting some newspapers as improvised fans) he sent Madame Plume de Matant to stack boxes of frozen fish fingers in the cold store.

Just because it was cold it didn't make the smell, which continued to leak squeakily all afternoon, any better. It just made it colder.

* * *

And it wasn't just Madame Plume de Matant who had a bad first day at the supermarket. (*What about Fizz?* I can hear you wondering. *It's his name on the front of the book, shouldn't you be talking about him a bit more? Hmm?* Well, to you impatient people I say: *patience.*) William Edgebottom, the off-duty Bongo Bongoton, was finding adjusting to the new job difficult too.

He had had the misfortune of being placed in the fresh fruit and veg section. Unlike Madame Plume de Matant, he wasn't in any danger of eating too much of the produce, and even if he had, he didn't have any vegetable intolerances, and so it wouldn't have been a tragedy of the cheese sort.

No, his problem was quite different.

He liked potatoes.

He liked potatoes very much.

(But not in a way that made him want to eat them raw. That would have been weird.)

He spent all morning stacking the potatoes under his care in neat pyramids, turning them this way and that until they showed off their most handsome faces. The way he piled them they became like works of art.

As customers wandered in the fruit and veg section, they noticed that the potatoes' eyes followed them round the room. That's how much of a work of art those spuds were.

Some people found it a bit unnerving. They hurried past, thinking, *Well, we had veg yesterday …*

But something worse than a few lost sales

happened when one brave customer walked up to the potato pyramid and lifted a nice fat King Edward from off the top.

He put it in his basket and was about to stroll off to examine the carrots and broccoli when he was knocked to the ground.

'Arthur!' a voice muttered in his ear.

The customer's name wasn't Arthur.

But the potato's was.

Arthur the King Edward.

William Edgebottom had rugby tackled the man (a rather impressive tackle for an elderly off-duty clown) and, rescuing the spud from the basket, he climbed to his feet.

'Arthur,' he murmured as he hugged the potato, dusted it down and placed it back perfectly positioned at the peak of the pinnacle of the pile. 'There you are, my precious, back with your friends. Don't worry, dears,' William went on, 'I shan't let anyone touch you. I shan't let them spoil your loveliness. My darling poes, my darling tays, my darling toes.'

Shortly before lunch he was sent, not to the cold store, but to work on the crisp aisle, among the packets filled with fried sliver

after fried sliver of his beloved vegetable friends.

He wept silently as he refilled the shelves.

Pinkbottle was proving (a) that he was the boss and wouldn't stand for any nonsense in his shop and (b) that he had an evil and unpleasant and nasty and rotten sense of justice in his punishments.

(Not everyone was having as bad a time of it as those two, however, even if no one was exactly *overjoyed* with their new roles. For example, Captain Fox Dingle was buttering scones in the supermarket's cafe, while Miss Tremble was making sure the broccoli faced the same way (the Captain liked a nice scone, and broccoli was Miss Tremble's seventh favourite vegetable). Emerald Sparkles was arranging soup cans in rows, while Mr Sparkles, her husband, was doing the same with cans of baked beans (it was easy enough, if not exactly thrilling). Mr Stump was in the stockroom moving boxes from here to there and then from there to here, and Mrs Stump was checking boxes of teabags to make sure they all weighed the same (dull but doable). Percy Late was in the crockery and household department dropping plates (at least it was something he'd had a lot of practice at; he was almost, you might say, an expert).

And the Ringmaster … well, he was out in the car park locked away inside his caravan, staring out of the drawn curtains and drinking too much lemon squash. (Pinkbottle hadn't bought his contract and technically he could have left at any time, but he was feeling guilty and sorry for himself and wanted to stay with his friends. However, he refused to come out of his caravan, so his moral support went somewhat unnoticed.))

All this while Fizz was carrying shopping for customers. (Both to their cars (aided by Dr Surprise's rainy day customer umbrella service), but also round the shop for little old ladies who didn't want to push a trolley, but who also didn't want to carry their own basket.) Fizz was good at his job, having the bulging muscles of a nascent strongman, and Mr Pinkbottle didn't need to punish him, although he sneered when he spoke to him.

Why, Fizz wondered, had the man bought the circus, only to let so many of them go? (Why had the Ringmaster agreed to sell up?)

Why had Pinkbottle made them work in his supermarket if he didn't like circus folk? (And he clearly didn't.) Surely it would make more sense, he thought, to just give jobs to normal people? It was all a mystery to Fizz, but he was working so hard in the shop, going to bed early and getting up just as early, that he was too tired to try to untangle the puzzle.

Talking to his mum and dad about it just led to a bad case of the grumbles and the 'Time for bed's. They were miserable like everyone else, and there was nothing they could do about it, not so long as Mr Pinkbottle owned their contracts.

I can, however, just to cheer you up among all this doom and gloom, let you know that we have now reached the bit in the story where the book began, way back in Chapter Four. (Although, technically, that was three weeks later than where we are, but what happened in those weeks in between now and then was just more of the same dreary, grumbly supermarket business. It was only after that scene in Chapter Four that the story *really* begins and things start to happen.)

Hold on to your hats, ladies and gentlemen, as we plunge into … the future!

CHAPTER FIVE

In which some people do work in a supermarket and in which a boy meets a boy he's met before

It was Thursday now. Thursday was half-day closing. The shop shut at two and the customers got the afternoon off.

Not so the staff.

They still had shelves to restock and floors to sweep, conveyor belts to oil and windows to clean, special offer labels to replace and dented tin cans to undent, sales targets to discuss and money to polish (Mr Pinkbottle liked the money he paid into the bank to be so spotless and shiny you wouldn't be ashamed to be seen in public with it).

But this Thursday was slightly different.

After the last customer had been shooed out and the front doors had been locked, Mr Pinkbottle let himself out of the back door and climbed into his car and drove off. Apparently, Fizz heard from Percy Late (who was now manning the fish counter), who'd heard from Miss Tremble, who'd overheard Mrs Leavings saying to Bertha Lotts (one of the dozen non-ex-circus supermarket employees) on the checkout, that Mr Pinkbottle was off on business in a neighbouring town, looking into a new supplier for tinned anchovies, pilchards and sardines, and she (Mrs Leavings) had been left in charge.

She loved being in charge. That much was clear. She waved her clipboard around and squinted at people as they worked. Sometimes she would tap her pen on a bit of paper and tut.

But she also loved her afternoon nap.

At three o'clock she retired to the little manager's office beside the staffroom to lie down on the sofa with an eye mask over her eyes and snore gently for an hour. (She did this every afternoon and signs were hung around the store informing customers of the need to keep the noise down.)

At two minutes past three Dr Surprise surprised Fizz by tapping him on the shoulder.

'Fizzlebert,' he said.

'Yes, Doctor,' Fizz answered.

'Shall we go out?'

'Out?'

'Yes, out.'

'Out where?'

'Just out.'

'Out?'

'Yes.'

'OK.'

To you or I 'going out' might not be that much of a big deal. I 'go out' most days. Sometimes I go to the shops and sometimes I have a walk up the park and sometimes I go into town. All sorts of things, because I like to keep life interesting. But Fizz hasn't been out for weeks. Life has been a dreary, repetitive, boring, repetitive, tiring, repetitive drudge of menial labour. It's been the same thing every day. Yawn.

But today looked to be different and Fizz's heart sang like a bird. (Not just any bird, but one of those ones that sings quite nicely, and that isn't in a cage.)

'Where will we go?' Fizz asked.

'Ah,' said the doctor. 'The world is our oyster. Just so long as we don't take too long and are back before Mrs Leavings wakes up. And just so long as my shellfish allergy doesn't flare up.'

'The library?' asked Fizz.

Dr Surprise nodded.

'We could,' he said. 'We could.'

'I'll have to get my card from the caravan,' Fizz said, 'but that won't take a minute.'

Ever since Fizz's first recorded adventure,

many books ago, way back in *Fizzlebert Stump: The Boy Who Ran Away from the Circus and Joined the Library* he'd been collecting library cards. Most towns that the circus visited had a library and either Dr Surprise or one of his parents would go with him to the library and sign up for a library card and then Fizz would borrow a couple of books. He had a special wallet in which he kept the library cards. He had seventeen of them and loved the sound as the wallet un-concertina-ed itself towards the floor, flapping and flipping and flopping (but *not* flupping or flepping, because they're not real words) as it unrolled.

'The library,' Dr Surprise said, 'is over by the park. You remember that, don't you?'

'What town are we in?' Fizz asked.

(He'd been here for weeks now but hadn't thought to ask. It hadn't been important when he only saw the inside of a supermarket.)

Dr Surprise told him the name of the town.

Fizz tapped at the library card in the very top slot of his unfolded card wallet.

He felt a little lump in his throat.

He was remembering the start of the summer. This was where he had got his first library card. It was the first library he had ever been in. Now in the autumn of the year they were back where they'd been six months before. (It had been a rather action-packed six months.)

He smiled sadly as he remembered how he'd stumbled into the library not knowing what it was for. He'd always liked reading books, but he'd never known where they came from. (He'd thought they came from shops! What an idiot!)

(By the way if you've not read that first Fizz book – *Fizzlebert Stump: The Boy Who Ran Away from the Circus and Joined the Library* – you ought to go and read it now (your local library might have a copy), because it's quite good. (Even if I say so myself. (Which I just did.)))

A lesson Fizz had learnt back then was to always tell at least one of your parents (preferably whichever one wasn't wearing clown make-up at the time) that you were going to the library so that, just in case you got kidnapped, they'd at least know where to start the search from.

So, he went up to his mum (who hadn't worn clown make-up for weeks, and who looked tired) and said, 'Dr Surprise is taking me to the library.'

She put down the baguette she was washing (she was working on the bakery counter) and said, 'Oh. Did Mr Pinkbottle say you could?'

Fizz said, 'Um.'

Luckily Fizz's mum took Fizz's, 'Um,' to be a, 'Yes, Mr Pinkbottle said we could go to the library,' and Fizz didn't correct her.

She went back to her baguettes and Fizz went back to the back door to find Dr Surprise waiting with an umbrella. (Not the same umbrella he used in the car park to protect customers (which had 'Pinkbottle's Supermarket' printed in huge garish letters), but a neat little black pop-up one that played 'God Save The Ringmaster of Ringmasters' whenever it came in contact with custard (which doesn't happen anywhere in this book, so don't hold your breath).)

The doctor pulled out his pocket watch.

'We need to be quick, Fizz,' he said. 'It's ten past now and it's a twelve-minute walk to the library. We'd best get going.'

And so they did. They got going.

It stopped raining as soon as Dr Surprise put the umbrella up and by the time they reached the library the sun was shining on them and the puddles were beginning to shrink, so Dr Surprise put the umbrella down again.

As they stepped through the automatic doors and breathed deep of the book-scented air the doctor looked at his watch and said, 'It's twenty-two minutes past three, Fizz. We need to be back before Mrs Leavings gets up at four o'clock. We need to leave here in thirty-one minutes. No later.' (He was so exact because he had a good watch that told you the seconds and everything (also the phase of the moon and whether it was raining or not (but that wasn't important right now)).)

'But,' said Fizz, lifting his finger as his head did the sums. 'In thirty-one minutes it will be seven minutes to four. It'll be three fifty-three. It took us twelve minutes to walk here. That won't be nearly enough time to get back.'

'Ah, but, Fizzlebert,' said Dr Surprise, removing his plastic moustache, polishing it on his sleeve and tapping the side of his nose with the hand that wasn't polishing, 'I know a short cut.'

(He also winked through his monocle, but

that sentence was quite long enough already, so I didn't mention it.)

Fizz considered saying something, but thought better of it. Time was limited and sometimes talking wasted it.

So instead he looked up at the brimming shelves of books. There were so many of them. So many! And every one was different. Every one opened a door into a different world, into a different adventure. In each one you met new people, made new friends, learnt new spells and words and jokes. He liked the ones with space robots in, and the ones with monsters. He didn't like ones with kissing in. Unless it was robots kissing monsters, maybe, although he'd never actually found a book in which that happened. Yet. (He hadn't quite given up hope.)

Dr Surprise and Fizz split up. The doctor went to look at the books on tricks and magic and other stuff like that, because that was what he liked. And Fizz went and sat on the floor in the children's section and started building piles of books around him, trying to decide which ones to take home.

Having a good book to read would make his lunch break so much better. If he could eat his yesterday sandwich (the staffroom was supplied with all the sandwiches that went out of date yesterday) while reading about space explosions and daring robberies and weird tentacles, then the yesterday sandwich might taste better.

After twenty-seven minutes of browsing books, of flicking through and checking that the pictures looked good, of reading the backs

and making sure the stories sounded good, of sniffing the paper to make sure it smelt how a real book ought to smell (you know the smell, the best library books or second-hand books have it), Fizz had whittled the big pile down to three books he really wanted: *Exploding Robots Fighting Stuff in Space* by Sylvia Speck-Winkle and Arnold B. Clerk, *The Penguin Who Flew (To Mars (and Back))* by Tyson Thumpracket and *Spinoza and the Curse of the Mummy from Beyond the Grave* by Brigadier Ryefoot-fforwerd (Rtd.).

Dr Surprise had one small paperback about carrots. ('For Flopples,' he explained.)

They queued up at the desk to check them out.

'Can I take these ones, please,' asked Fizz, who was very polite, especially when facing a librarian who had once loaned him some books that he had never returned (although, that was when he was using another name, for various reasons too complicated to go into right now – again read *Fizzlebert Stump: The Boy Who Ran Away from the Circus and Joined the Library* if you haven't already and didn't go and immediately do it when I told you to earlier).

'Yes,' croaked Miss Toad, the librarian.

She didn't recognise him, it seemed.

She noisily licked her inky fingertips and flipped the pages of the first book to find the front page. She zapped the bar code with a laser thing and then slammed an inky rubber stamp down on the flap of paper, leaving a dark blue smudged inky date at the bottom of a list of other dark blue inkily smudged dates. Fizz could read none of them.

Once she had scanned and stamped the other two books and handed Fizz his library card back he let Dr Surprise step up to the counter.

'Oh,' said the doctor. 'I've got it somewhere. Um …'

He patted his pockets looking for his wallet.

Fizz sat down on one of the chairs over by the automatic doors. He let his feet swing underneath him and balanced his little pile of books on his knee.

Oh, he felt better than he had for ages. Just getting out of the supermarket had buoyed his heart up, just smelling the fresh air of the world outside made him smile.

Having new books to read made him laugh. While he'd been sat there dipping in and out of all the borrowable books he'd even forgotten Mr Pinkbottle for a moment.

'Fizzlebert?' said a voice.

He looked up, snapped out of his daydream.

He was looking at a boy who was looking at him looking at him looking at him.

'Kevin?' said Fizz.

'Yeah,' said Kevin.

Kevin had been the last person Fizz had expected to see. (Actually that's not true, but to accurately tell you the name of the last person Fizz expected to see I'd have to run through the other seven billion or so people on earth going, 'He didn't expect to see this one or this one …' until I reached the last one, who was probably living in an uncontacted tribe deep in a rainforest somewhere, and, frankly, however much I like you, I don't have the time or space to do that.)

'What are you doing here?' Fizz asked, while I was talking to you inside that last set of brackets.

Kevin looked around him.

'It's a library, Fizz,' he said. 'I'm bringing some books back. But what are *you* doing here?'

'It's a library, Kevin. I'm borrowing some books.'

'That makes sense.'

Fizz and Kevin had first met under very different circumstances which I won't tell you about except to say it involved a sticky situation, some nefarious old people, a lot of housework, one lion, two parrots and a borrowed pocket watch.

'You doing another show?' Kevin asked, pointing over his shoulder with his thumb out at the outside.

'No,' said Fizz, feeling misery well up from somewhere underneath him. 'We're not really in the circus any more.' He gulped. 'We're working at … Pinkbottle's Supermarket.'

'Oh,' said Kevin.

When Fizz's circus had visited his town before, Kevin had got to help Fizz with the show, because of the adventure they'd had together. The sparkle in his eyes, that dimmed as he heard Fizz's words, suggested to Fizz that Kevin might've been thinking that he (Kevin) might've got to do the act with him

(Fizz) again, even though Fizz knew that he did a different act to the act he had done when he first met Kevin and that Kevin probably wouldn't be very good at it since it was a strongman act, not a 'put your head in the mouth of a lion' act, and Kevin was just an ordinary boy without super-strength and, boy, has this sentence got long and I'm running out of breath even though I'm only typing it and not reading it out loud but for anyone who is reading it out loud, I'm sorry.

'Yeah,' said Fizz, agreeing with Kevin's disappointed, 'Oh.'

'It's just that I saw the Big Top,' Kevin went on, 'and then I saw you and I thought, "Aha!" like you do.'

'Big Top?' Fizz said.

'In the park,' Kevin said. It was what he'd been pointing at with his thumb.

That was interesting news, Fizz thought. If there was another circus in town, maybe they'd be able to help out. After all, circus people, even ones from rival circuses, stuck together when shove came to push.

If only he could get a message to them somehow, maybe their Ringmaster could buy their contracts off Mr Pinkbottle or *something*. Fizz didn't know what exactly, but he knew the circus would only be there for a few days, so he had to act fast. But first –

'Fizzlebert,' said Dr Surprise, stepping up and peering at Kevin. 'We need to hurry. It's seven minutes to four.'

'Gotta go,' Fizz said to Kevin, apologetically.

'It was nice to see you again,' Kevin said.

'You too,' said Fizz.

'Maybe I'll see you in the shop,' Kevin said, as Fizz and the doctor made their way outside. 'Pinkbottle's?'

'Yeah,' said Fizz over his shoulder.

And then they were gone, away into the

gathering gloom, taking Dr Surprise's short cut back to the supermarket.

This had been an interesting and useful trip out, Fizz thought. There were books under his arm and a tickle of hope somewhere just to the side of his heart. (Either that or some of lunch's yesterday sandwich was coming back to visit.)

And that's where we'll leave them, scuttling through alleyways heading home on this ordinary Thursday afternoon. And we'll find out what happens when they get back to the shop in the next chapter, because that's what happens next. And trust me, it's quite a good bit with a lot of shouting in.

CHAPTER SIX

In which an escape is thwarted and in which further punishment is meted out

By the time they arrived back in the supermarket, creeping into the car park where their caravans were squeezed up together, hoping to not be noticed, it was raining again. It was also four minutes past five.

They had left the library at seven minutes to four.

Dr Surprise's short cut hadn't *quite* lived up to its name. Not exactly. Not entirely. Not satisfactorily. Even the doctor was disappointed with it, and he was usually quite cheerful when things went wrong.

'Oh, but Flopples will be worried,' he'd squeaked as they'd stood and looked at a small oak tree they'd passed three times already. 'She does fuss if I'm not home when I say I will be.'

'It's not Flopples I'm worried about,' Fizz had said. 'It's Mrs Leavings. What if she's woken up from her nap? She'll be furious.'

Fortunately, when they arrived back, it turned out he hadn't needed to worry about Mrs Leavings at all. She was awake, but she wasn't angry. She simply tapped her pen on her clipboard and smiled at them.

Not angry at all.

Mr Pinkbottle, on the other hand, was a different kettle of rapidly boiling water (full of dead fish) entirely.

He was waiting in the doorway. His toe was tapping as if he had a really flipping furious song in his head.

'Where have you been!?' he thundered.

It was a surprisingly thundery voice for a man so short and pointy-faced.

The pointy face was red like a balloon. A red one.

Fizz didn't say anything. He just stood under Dr Surprise's umbrella as rain fell around him. He was cold. His feet were soaking wet (thanks to the 'short cut', which at one point had involved fording a shallow river) and his shoulder ached from the incident with the squirrels (which I don't have room to tell you about).

'We went to the library,' Dr Surprise said, with surprising calm.

Mr Pinkbottle turned slightly redder (like a tomato that had just heard a rude joke) before bellowing, 'I do not pay you to go to the library!!'

'But,' said Dr Surprise, meekly.

'No ifs,' yelled Mr Pinkbottle, irrelevantly.

'But,' said Dr Surprise, as if he were about to argue, really quietly.

'No buts,' yelled Mr Pinkbottle, relevantly.

Rain dripped down the back of Fizz's neck, under his shirt collar.

'You two abandoned your posts,' Mr Pinkbottle said, talking more quietly now. 'You left everyone else to do your work. You are not team players. I am shocked and saddened and appalled and embarrassed by your behaviour. I take you in, out of the kindness of my heart. Mrs Leavings and I welcome you into our dear supermarket family, this family we have built and that we *love*. And what thanks do we get? Nothing. Nothing. Nothing. You two just spit all our kindness back in our faces.'

He shook his head as if he were genuinely saddened (even though Fizz didn't believe a word of it).

Behind him Mrs Leavings grinned and looked down at her clipboard.

'Bonding,' Mr Pinkbottle said eventually. 'That's what we need. Something that will make you feel at one with the family.'

Mrs Leavings leant forward and whispered something in his ear.

'Oh yes,' he said. 'That'll do.'

Fizz and Dr Surprise were sent to their caravans without any supper and told to report extra early the next morning for their new assignments.

Fizz spent the evening reading one of his new books which wasn't as good as he'd hoped it would be. (But sometimes that happens, doesn't it? The publisher puts a really exciting cover on a book, with spaceships and unicorns and explosions and princesses and *everything*, but then when you start reading it you discover it's actually about fourteenth-century Flemish tax law. Of course, by that point you've already paid for the book and the joke's on you. (Which is one of the reasons libraries are so useful: no money has changed hands.))

When his mum and dad came in they didn't *exactly* ignore him, but they were tired and preoccupied and *more or less* ignored him.

'Mum, Dad!' Fizz said excitedly. 'There's another circus in town, over in the park. It's only twelve minutes' walk away. Unless you take Dr Surprise's short cut,' he added. 'We should go and ask them if we can join up.'

'Can't this wait until tomorrow, Fizz?' his mum said, brushing breadcrumbs out of her uniform. 'I'm tired, love.'

'Dad,' Fizz said. 'I met Kevin in the library. You remember Kevin?'

'You shouldn't have gone off without telling anyone,' his dad said, not angrily, but yawningly. 'You could've got us all into trouble.'

Why had his dad become so boring? His

mum was just the same – instead of being clowny and silly and funny and spilling custard and dropping teapots, juggling balls and feathers that clanged as if they were made of lead, she was always looking over her shoulder. She seemed to be *worried about the consequences*, worried about what Mr Pinkbottle *might say*.

It was as if their anarchic souls had been sucked out through their noses and sealed inside Canopic jars (with the brains and hearts of dead pharaohs). There was no fight in them. They just did what they were told.

'But he has our contracts, Fizz,' they'd said, as if that were some sort of explanation (which, of course, it was). 'We can't risk upsetting the apple cart or who knows where we'll end up.' And then they'd shrug and go back to whatever menial bit of supermarket shelf-stacking or floor-sweeping or trolley-polishing they'd been doing.

It was as if his funny, exciting, caring, happy parents had been taken away and replaced with robots that looked like them, but with grey bags under their eyes and voices emptied out of feeling. It sank Fizz's heart like an iceberg. (Not like how an iceberg sinks a ship, but like how an iceberg floats. Nine-tenths of it sinks, while the little bit sticks up out of the water, like a tiny reminder of hope.)

(He knew his mum was, secretly, worried, however, because she'd started sleep-eating. Sometimes Fizz would wake in the night to see her nibbling cheese, or making a soufflé, or drinking custard from the packet … while snoring and with her eyes fast shut. But if he tried to tell her, in the morning, she denied everything and said there was nothing to worry about and told him he must've dreamt it. But he hadn't.)

Well, if *they* weren't going to fight against what had happened to them, it would be up to him.

He had to get to the other circus. He had to get help.

And so, later that night, when everyone was asleep, Fizzlebert Stump ran away.

'Where do you think you're going?' hissed Mrs Leavings as Fizz climbed out of the caravan window. 'Get back to bed. Now!'

Fizz climbed back through the caravan window and lay down on his bed.

He hadn't expected her to be sat by the supermarket's back door.

It was as if she was on guard. She'd had a steaming mug of coffee (he had smelt it) and had been reading a magazine by the light of a little torch (he had seen it).

Fizz could've fought her or made a run for it, maybe, but that wouldn't have been much good. Not really. It wasn't that he wanted to *escape*. He wanted to *get help*. It wasn't just him that was in trouble, it was the whole lot of them. He couldn't abandon his mum and dad and Dr Surprise and Percy Late and Emerald Sparkles and her husband and the others.

He lay on his bed with his eyes open and his brain ticking through impossible plans and stupid ideas until his eyes shut of their own accord and he began to dream.

The only dream he remembered in the morning was the one where he was being shaken awake.

Fizz was shaken awake.

Mr Pinkbottle was in their caravan. It was still dark outside. His dad was snoring. His mum was snoring (even though she always assured Fizz that she didn't).

'Get up, Stump,' the supermarket manager said, quietly but firmly but quietly.

Fizz sat up.

'What time is it?'

'Time for work,' Mr Pinkbottle sneered. 'Get your uniform on and be outside in three minutes.'

Fizz was dressed and outside in two and a half.

'Here's your brush,' Mr Pinkbottle said. 'There is cleaning to do.'

He led Fizz inside the building, through the storehouse at the back and into the shop itself.

He pointed at the floor.

There were marks on the tiles where the

wheels of trolleys had got stuck and scraped along and where people had trodden mud and muck in from the street and where Mr Pinkbottle had just spilt a large tub of rice.

'The store opens in two hours,' Mr Pinkbottle said, 'and it'd better look spotless. Or else.'

And with that he strode off to his office, leaving Fizz alone with a large scattering of rice, a dirty floor the size of a supermarket and a brush.

The brush, I didn't mention before, was the size of the sort you use to clean your teeth, that is to say: it was a very small brush.

(He also had a tiny dustpan to go with it and a black bin bag.)

Fizz grumbled to himself but there was nothing he could do, not right now.

He lowered himself to his knees and began sweeping the rice up. He'd do that first and then he'd scrub at the mud and the marks, but he didn't have any soapy water or anything, just elbow grease (which was available in tins on Aisle B, along with tartan paint and glass hammers).

He tipped the tiny dustpan full of rice into the black bin bag and then scooped up some more.

After a while the bin bag began to grow heavy, as Fizz shuffled forward on his knees across the floor.

After another while the bin bag was practically full.

It had taken ages, but all the rice was up off the floor.

So were the lentils, the barley and the dried

kidney beans which had all also been *accidentally* knocked over just in front of Fizz.

Mr Pinkbottle walked up, his shoes clacking on the tiles.

'That bag looks almost full,' he said. (There was no, 'Well done.') He prodded it with his toe, and then he called, 'Mr Stump, coo-ee!'

Fizz's dad appeared from around the corner of some shelves. His supermarket uniform bulged across his muscles, the seams gaping and the buttons looking worryingly close to bursting off in all directions. He didn't smile when he saw Fizz.

'Move this sack.'

Mr Pinkbottle pointed and Mr Stump bent and lifted.

'For the bin?' he asked.

'Yes, yes,' Mr Pinkbottle said, and then, as Fizz's dad turned and began lumbering towards the back doors, he said, 'No, stop!'

Mr Stump stopped.

Fizz looked up.

'This won't do,' Mr Pinkbottle said. 'Look at this. This bag is damaged. You, boy, you must have damaged this bag.'

Fizz couldn't see anything wrong with the black bag. It was keeping everything in, which is all it had to do.

The supermarketeer tapped on his clipboard with his pen and then, when Fizz said nothing, pointed at the bin bag.

'Look here, there's a hole.'

'I don't see –' began Fizz, just as Mr Pinkbottle jabbed his pen through the plastic and suddenly a sackful of beans, rice and

lentils spilt, like a very dry waterfall, across the floor.

Mr Pinkbottle snapped out a tiny mousetrap-like laugh, before leaning down and hissing, 'You'd better get sweeping, boy. The shop opens in twenty minutes and this is a health and safety hazard. And it's all your fault! What if an inspector came today? Hmm? HMMM?'

'Now then,' Mr Stump said, turning round with the deflated black bag flapping on his shoulder as if he were a particularly rubbish superhero. 'It wasn't Fizz's fault and I won't have you shouting at my son like that.'

He stepped towards the supermarket man, towering over him and casting a strongman's shadow over his face.

At last! Fizz thought, Dad's got some of

his old self back. He's woken up!

He was about to whoop with joy as the nasty manager was lifted up by his lapels and dangled in the air, but it never happened.

As Mr Stump loomed, Mr Pinkbottle flicked through the papers on his clipboard until he found the one he wanted and showed it to the strongman.

'I think you'll find,' he said, 'that if you lay a finger on my lapel I'll be forced to sell this contract of yours to a pal of mine who runs a florist's shop in Australia. There you go, Mr Stump, flying off down under to cut flowers, with no family beside you, because they'll still be mine. It's a great opportunity. We can do it now, if you'd like to come to my office. Just a quick phone call and a simple signature, that's all it will take. Hmm?'

Mr Stump cowered.

'Sorry,' he mumbled.

Then he said, 'Fizz, you'd best clear all this up.'

'Well done, Mr Stump,' said Mr Pinkbottle. 'Back to stacking marshmallows with you. Go on, go.'

Fizz's dad gave him an embarrassed nod, not looking in his eyes, and slinked away around the shelving unit, back to the marshmallow aisle.

Fizz, defeated and not knowing what else to do, knelt back down and started scooping up the rice and beans and lentils and a family-sized tubful of couscous that had also found itself accidentally spilt among the rest.

'No, no, no!' snapped Mr Pinkbottle. 'Not like that. The doors will be opening soon and I can't have an ugly little boy sweeping in the middle of the shop like this. 'Let me think. Oh! I've got it.'

When the shop opened not a single customer looked at Fizz and thought, *Oh what a poor boy, forced to do pointless tasks by a brutal shopkeeper*. And they didn't think this because they didn't see Fizz, even though he was there, right in front of them.

And they didn't see Fizz because they saw a small gorilla (or a small person in a gorilla suit, because most people can tell the difference between a real gorilla in a supermarket and someone in a suit hired from a fancy dress shop. They're customers, not idiots, after all).

Beside the small gorilla-boy with the tiny

dustpan and brush was a sign that said: *Pay a Pound and Spill Some Rice! – Watch the Ape Tidy Up! – All Proceeds to Charity!* And people were doing as the sign suggested. They paid their pound to Mrs Leavings and tipped a packet of rice on the floor and watched as the 'ape' scuttled forward and began sweeping up.

And that was how Fizz spent his day, hot and bothered, and unable to escape. Always that woman with her clipboard and her rattling charity bucket. Always more jolly customers laughing and smiling as they tipped rice and pasta, lentils and quinoa on the floor, thinking they were doing some good in the world through their charitable contributions. (I'll let you imagine what sort of charity Mr Pinkbottle might support. Let's just say, it wasn't one that was kind to animals, children or classic cars of the 1930s.)

You might be thinking, '*Shouldn't Fizz's punishment for having 'run away' (and come back again) have been* funnier? *This book is sort of a comedy, after all.*' But I'm afraid Mr Pinkbottle didn't have much of a sense of humour. He wasn't like Miss Trunchbull, for example, in Roald Dahl's book *Matilda*, who mixed her nastiness with appropriate and brutally funny punishments. The difference, of course, is that Mr Dahl was telling you a story that he'd made up out of his head, whereas I'm stuck relating to you the truth of the matter. I could make it funnier, but as Fizz would tell you if you sat down and spoke to him, it just wasn't very funny. And I'm not going to lie to you. I have never lied to you before and never will. You know that.

To give you an idea of how nasty Mr Pinkbottle was I'll tell you what Dr Surprise has been doing all this time, because, after all, he was out of the supermarket when he shouldn't have been too.

Dr Surprise spent his day working on the butcher's counter, but there'd been a mix up with the deliveries and the lorry that brought the meat in hadn't had any beef or pork or buffalo or kangaroo or venison or bacon or veal or boar or ostrich or lamb. All they'd had was rabbit. Lots and lots of rabbit. Rabbit chops and rabbit sausages. Rabbit burgers and rabbit mince. Rabbit ears and rabbit feet. Rabbit steaks and rabbit offal. And if you don't know what offal is, then you've probably got good, kind and loving parents.

Dr Surprise loved rabbits. Just not like this.

(See? Not a *funny* punishment, but one that only someone as cruel and nasty as Mr Pinkbottle would come up with for a man who had performed nightly (with matinees on Saturday and Sunday) for years with a rabbit called Flopples in his hat.)

CHAPTER SEVEN

In which a boy runs away to the cicrus and in which an act of subterfuge is uncovered

It's now somewhere between five and five thirty in the evening on that same Friday.

Fizzlebert is running through dark streets, retracing his way to the library.

Fizz is hurrying, his heart is beating as if someone's chasing him, though he doesn't think anyone is. Not yet, anyway.

He slips and slides round one final corner and the lights of the library are there before him, glowing out into the dark autumnal street, warm and inviting and safe.

But that's not where he's going. He runs past the library, past Miss Toad (who he sees crunching a biro between her teeth behind her desk), past the hundred thousand books, the hundred thousand other stories and on, on further into this new chapter all of his own.

He's in the park now, running on wet grass.

Before him are the lights of a circus.

He can see the Big Top, he can see the lights on in people's caravan windows and the dull yellow glow of buzzing lightbulbs strung between them.

The one thought in his head is: I must get help. I must find their Ringmaster.

He slows down. He stops running.

He looks at the Big Top again.

When you've worked in the circus your whole life you can recognise a Big Top immediately: it's where all your most exciting moments happen; it's where you come together as a big family and make the world a better and brighter place; it's where you show off. It's the signpost that means you never get lost. Wherever you go the Big Top towers over everything, like the Eiffel Tower in Paris: it's a landmark that will always let you find your way home.

And in the same way that an expert can tell the difference between the Eiffel Tower and the Leaning Tower of Pisa just by looking at them, so too can a circus expert tell which circus's Big Top they're looking at just by looking at it too.

Fizz looked, trying to work out whose Big Top it was. As he looked the thought came that there was something odd about this one.

It wasn't, he realised, as *Big* as the Big Top he was used to.

In fact it looked, now he *really* looked at it, more like a *Medium* Top.

Then it hit him: he knew whose circus this was.

There was only one circus on the circuit that had a Medium Top and that was *Neil Coward's Famous Cicrus*. (A long time ago the misspelling had been painted on the side of Neil Coward's wagon, and it had proved cheaper to keep than to change. Nowadays he

explained to people that it was the 'continental' spelling. (It isn't.))

Fizz's heart sank and then bobbed up again.

It sank because *Coward's* was (to be quite blunt) the most rubbish circus he knew of. Its performers were either so new they'd not had time to practise, or so old and tired they'd long since passed their peak. *Coward's* was the place you ended up when you'd run out of talent, luck or custard.

The Ringmaster, Neil Coward himself, was (Fizz remembered from the one time he'd met him) a bit of a monster. Not a scary monster, but one of those ones made out of jelly that sit in the corner of a dungeon wobbling and waiting for an adventurer to trip up and fall into them. He was wet and weak and giggled at things no one else ever found funny.

More importantly he was poor. His cicrus was so rubbish it didn't draw big crowds and didn't make big bucks.

Fizz had hoped, secretly, that he might find a Ringmaster who'd go to Mr Pinkbottle and make such a good offer to buy the contracts that the horrid little supermarketeer would be unable to refuse. But that wasn't going to happen now. Not a chance. Not in a million years. (Not that it would matter in a million years, since Fizz and his mum and dad would be long dead by then, and, also, the contracts only had eleven years to run before they were free of them anyway.)

But, I said Fizz's heart also bobbed up when he realised which circus the cicrus in front of him was, didn't I? That was because he knew someone who worked for Ringmaster Coward who *wasn't* rubbish.

At the end of the summer Fizz's circus and *Neil Coward's Famous Cicrus* had parked up in the same field for a while and Fizz had met a girl called Alice Crudge. This is all recorded in a book called *Fizzlebert Stump and the Girl Who Lifted Quite Heavy Things*.

Like Fizz she was a junior strongperson, although her dad had had her doing a Flower Arranging act for reasons of his own. Needless to say, by the end of that book she had proved herself to be a brilliant young strongwoman and he'd grudgingly allowed her to begin lifting quite heavy things as her act.

(And if you've read that book you'll be

thinking right now, '*But at the end of the story she was offered a place in* La Spectacular De La Spectacular De La Rodriguez' Silent Circus Of Dreams, *a far bigger and better circus than Neil Coward's Famous Cicrus.*' '*Surely*,' a friend of yours who's been reading your mind over your shoulder, might think, '*Fizz isn't stupid enough to have forgotten that?*'

Well, you can tell your friend, that what he or she doesn't know is that Fizz had had a letter from Alice only a month before this book began, saying that her dad had had an argument with Ringmaster Rodriguez over the appropriate number of ruffles on a dancing dog's tutu (he'd been working in the costume department) and they'd had to leave and had gone back and joined *Coward's* once again because no one else had room for a brilliant stronggirl and her cantankerous and hard-to-get-on-with father.

So there.)

Fizz thought that even though this circus was no good for actually rescuing his friends from the supermarket, it would still have been nice to see Alice again. (That's one of the annoying things about travelling circuses: you can make friends with people in them, but you'll very rarely end up in the same place at the same time. It can be lonely, with or without the occasional letter.)

There was only one thing to do, wasn't there?

Fizz went among the caravans and knocked on the first door he came to.

'Hello?' said a person dressed as a cloud.

'Hello,' said Fizz (he was never surprised

by people dressed as clouds). 'I was wondering if Alice was around. Alice Crudge? Do you know which caravan is hers?'

'The Crudges are just over there,' said the cloud, pointing at a caravan just over there.

Fizz said, 'Thank you,' and went just over there and knocked again.

'Hello?' said another person dressed as a cloud.

'Hello,' Fizz answered. 'I wondered if Alice was home?'

'Hmmph,' said the cloud.

'Fizzlebert?' said Alice from behind him.

'Alice,' said Fizz, turning round to face her.

The caravan door was slammed shut.

'Don't mind Dad,' Alice said. 'He's just grumpy because the Ringmaster's got him playing a cloud in tonight's Zeppelin Race.'

'I thought he was a plate spinner?' Fizz said.

'Oh, he is, but we've run out of plates, so he's got to pull his weight elsewhere tonight.'

Fizz said nothing. His heart was thumping in his chest because he'd found another of his friends. The fact that he was no closer to freeing his family from Pinkbottle's grip was forgotten for the moment as Alice smiled at him.

When he still said nothing she filled the silence by saying, 'What are you doing here?'

Meanwhile, back in the supermarket, at exactly the same time, Fizzlebert-in-a-gorilla-suit was scooping up yogurt with his dustpan and slopping it into a black plastic bin bag.

Mr Pinkbottle watched and tipped a packet

of Nicey Ricey breakfast cereal on to the tiled floor.

'Ladies and gentlemen,' he said to the gathered crowd, 'look at how quickly the little monkey works, eager to raise money for *charity*.'

He nudged Mrs Stump who stood by his side and she rattled a bucket.

People dropped change in and the bucket rattled some more.

Mrs Stump looked sad.

Maybe the bucket reminded her of happier times, with custard and trousers and laughter. Or maybe she felt powerless watching her son being humiliated in a gorilla costume in the name of fundraising.

Back to the cicrus!

During that 'meanwhile' Fizz had explained to Alice everything that had happened so far. And he'd told her his plan, how he wanted to find someone to buy the contracts off Pinkbottle and take them all back to where they ought to be.

'But,' said Alice, sitting on the steps of her caravan, 'you're looking at it all wrong.

You've not asked yourself the obvious questions, Fizz! You won't get anywhere unless you ask the right questions.'

Fizz knew that she was right. She had a funny nose that bent slightly to the left and he had liked her almost from the moment they'd met. Of course she was right! She'd helped make the ending of that other book turn out all right, using her brain *and* her brawn. He knew he should listen to her.

'What do you mean?' he said.

'You're all about this, "Find someone to buy the contracts", when you should be asking, "Why did the Ringmaster sell the contracts in the first place?". I mean, that's not a normal thing to do, is it? When have you ever heard of a Ringmaster selling up his whole circus?'

'What about Ringmaster Moondust of *Moondust & Daughters Interstellar Circus of Surprises?*'

'Well, apart from that time.'

'*Abner Palmer's Circus of Bees?*'

'And that one.'

Fizz couldn't think of any others so Alice continued.

'What you ought to ask is, "What does this supermarket bloke have that *made* the Ringmaster sell up?"'

'A lot of money?'

'I don't believe that,' Alice said. 'Yours is … was … a *good* circus. People actually came to see you. They bought tickets. You weren't struggling, were you?'

'No,' Fizz had to admit. Ticket sales had been strong recently.

'So, it's not the money, or not *just* the money. You say you overheard the supermarket bloke say he'd spent five hundred quid. Well, that's not a fraction of what the circus was worth. Something else is going on here.'

'But what?' asked Fizz.

She looked around, as if to make sure they weren't being listened to, tapped the

side of her nose and whispered one word: 'Blackmail.'

'Blackmail?' said Fizz.

'Blackmail,' she repeated.

'Blackmail,' said Fizz.

Alice looked at him and squinted.

'You *do* know what blackmail is, don't you?'

'Of course I do,' said Fizz. 'But do you?'

'Yeah,' said Alice. 'It's when you make someone pay you money or do something for you, because you know some special secret they don't want shared. You threaten to expose their secret if they don't do what you say.'

'Exactly,' said Fizz, nodding. 'So, you reckon Pinkbottle's blackmailing the Ringmaster?'

'Why else would he sell up?'

Fizz stroked his chin and wished he had a beard.

Let's change places again! Back to the supermarket!

It was six o'clock.

The last customer was hurried out of the doors by Mrs Leavings and her clipboard.

Silence descended.

Mr Pinkbottle snatched the bucket from Mrs Stump.

It jangled and clinked.

It was heavy. He smiled as he hefted its weight in his hand.

'All right,' he said. 'You're done for now. You can get out of that costume and go help Ms Sparkles in the laundry. Them uniforms won't wash themselves, will they?'

The gorilla-boy-that-can't-actually-be-Fizz-because-he's-at-the-cicrus didn't move.

It looked at Mr Pinkbottle and then at Mrs Stump and then up and down the aisle as if looking for something. Not seeing what it was looking for it slumped where it sat and gave a big sigh, followed by an 'Uh-oh' noise.

Are you getting dizzy yet? Confused? Hang on to your hat one last time.

Meanwhile! At the same time! Back in the cicrus!

Fizz and Alice had come up with a plan to find out what Mr Pinkbottle was holding over the Ringmaster's head, blackmailwise. (Naturally I'm not going to tell you, right now. Patience, after all, is my middle name.

(Actually it's Francis, but that's not important right now.))

'I've got to go,' Fizz said, looking at his watch and seeing the time.

'You can't stay for the show?' Alice said.

Wild horses couldn't have dragged Fizz to see a show at *Neil Coward's Famous Cicrus*, even if it did have Alice in it, but he didn't say that. Instead he said something else, which was also the truth.

'If I don't get back quick Kevin's gonna be in trouble.'

'Kevin?'

'He's a friend of mine. He –'

'What act's he do?'

'Kevin? He doesn't do an act. He's … he's *normal*.'

'Oh,' said Alice.

'But he's wearing a gorilla suit cleaning things up off the floor for charity.'

'Oh,' said Alice. 'Why's he doing that?'

'He's a friend.'

Fizz looked at his watch. It had just gone six and he knew the doors to the supermarket would be shut by now. He was already too late to get back in time. He just had to hope that Kevin wouldn't have had to take the mask off yet. Maybe Pinkbottle was busy elsewhere, or maybe Kevin would think of something.

'He came in the shop after school and I managed to convince Mr Pinkbottle to let me have a toilet break and while no one was looking we swapped places. And I escaped. Only now I'm afraid he's going to get caught. Again.'

'Well, you'd best run,' Alice said.

And Fizz did run, back through the park and past the library, in the hope that his friend wasn't in the trouble you and I know he's probably already in.

This chapter began with Fizz running and it will end with him running. That's what we call, in the book-writing business, 'a symmetrical structure' or 'a mirror-image opener-closer technique' or maybe 'a chapter in which a boy runs in and runs out'. I don't know really. I never took any classes to help me do this stuff. I don't know the technical terms. I just write it down as it occurs to me.

In the next chapter things get tricky (trick*ier*), but I won't spoil it for you by telling you all about it now; instead you can just go and read the next chapter which tells you everything you need to know about what happens in Chapter Eight.

CHAPTER EIGHT

In which a boy falls over a dustbin and in which a single chocolate bar is eaten by three people

We pick up the story with Mr Pinkbottle clutching a bucket of unethically earned 'charity' donations and looming over a boy-in-a-gorilla-suit, demanding that he get changed and go help Emerald Sparkles, the former circus knife thrower, in the laundry, washing and starching and ironing all the supermarket uniforms (and, presumably, shortly, the gorilla suit).

'Come on, Fizz,' Mrs Stump said. 'Let's get you out of this costume. You can have a sandwich before the laundry.' (She looked at Mr Pinkbottle as she said this, and he scowled meaningfully.) 'Your dad found some out-of-date fish paste which Mr Pinkbottle's let us have.'

The boy-in-a-gorilla-suit slowly climbed to his feet.

'Quicker than that,' Mr Pinkbottle snapped. (He wanted to go and count the money while he had his dinner.) 'Hurry up. Five minutes, then I want him in the laundry. Understood?'

Mrs Stump took the gorilla by the hand and hurried it off towards the back door.

'Oh,' she grumbled under her breath as they went. 'Oh, that man.'

Once they'd gone through the storeroom and out into the dark car park, climbed the steps up to the caravan and shut the door behind them, she lifted the gorilla head off the head of a boy she thought was her son and looked into the face of a boy who she suddenly suspected *wasn't* her son.

'Hello,' she said, trying not to look too surprised.

'Hello,' said Kevin, who wasn't surprised at all. (He'd known he was him all day.)

Mrs Stump dropped the gorilla head on the table and rubbed the bridge of her nose.

'Why aren't you Fizz?' she asked. 'I was *expecting* Fizz.'

'Therein,' said Kevin, who liked to begin explanations by saying 'therein', a word he'd learnt during the summer holidays, 'hangs a tale.'

He explained and Mrs Stump shook her head wearily.

As Kevin came to the end of his explanation there was a loud knocking on the caravan door. (Actually 'knocking' is too kind and gentle a word to describe the noise. It was a thunderous hammering like a truck driver smacking the bottom of a particularly claggy bottle of ketchup in a roadside cafe full of hundreds of other burly truck drivers all banging their bottle bottoms too.)

'Yes?' called Mrs Stump.

'He's late,' shouted Mr Pinkbottle from outside. 'If he's not out here in ten seconds I'm going to dock his wages *and* put your husband to work on the soft fruit section.'

'Oh dear,' whispered Mrs Stump.

'It's OK,' said Kevin. 'I'll do it.' (He wanted to help Fizz out. He liked Fizz and even though they'd only written a couple of letters to one another since their first adventure Kevin had treasured them.

Although being kidnapped just once by an old lady had taught him to be wary of going off with strangers again, and although he was glad he'd learnt that lesson, he was still a bit bored just doing his homework and watching telly and playing football and going to his Junior Knitters Kitten Knitting Club. Secretly he'd been longing for an adventure of the sort Fizz had written to him about and this was his big chance (possibly his *only* chance) to be a part of one.

That was why he'd come to the supermarket in the first place. He'd been sure, when they'd met in the library, that something was going on, and he'd come to see if he could help. His mum and dad would probably be out looking for him by now, maybe they'd even have already phoned the police, but *Kevin* knew he wasn't lost. He wasn't worried. He'd go home to them when he was ready. In the meantime it was *adventure time*.

(I'd like to point out at this point that Kevin wasn't thinking entirely straight. His mum and dad *were* worried he'd gone missing again and they *had* indeed phoned the police and it was *very* serious because Kevin hadn't told them he was planning on having an adventure and staying out late. Just because *he* knew where he was didn't mean he *wasn't* missing and it was wrong of him to, knowingly, cause his parents so much worry. Especially on a night like this when their favourite programme, *Stop! Look! Redecorate!*, was on telly.))

Mrs Stump looked down at the boy who had just volunteered to take Fizz's place in the laundry, to save his friend from getting in trouble, and immediately spotted a problem.

So long as Kevin kept the gorilla suit on he was the spitting image of Fizz-in-a-gorilla-suit (of, in fact, almost *any* boy-in-a-gorilla-suit), but the moment he took it off he looked like *an entirely different boy*. Mr Pinkbottle might be mean and cruel, but he wasn't an idiot and he would spot the deception within, literally, minutes. (A half-hour at the most. Unless he was distracted, say, maybe by an amusing pigeon or a hard sum or a bucket of cash, in which case I'd say … forty-six minutes at the outside.) And *then* they'd all be in trouble. Again.

'I can't let you do that,' she said.

'Awww,' complained Kevin.

'Hurry up!' yelled Mr Pinkbottle.

'Just a minute!' Mrs Stump shouted back. 'He's getting changed.'

She had to think! Think! Think think think! *Think* …

Try as she might she couldn't see a solution. She considered getting her clown make-up out and painting Kevin's face and claiming Fizz had developed a rash, but that wouldn't explain why the boy's hair was a different colour. Or she could put the gorilla head back on and explain that Fizz was stuck inside the suit, but she knew that wouldn't work. All it would take was one yank by Mr Pinkbottle and the head would come off again. Deception discovered!

Argh! There was nothing she could do.

Mr Stump would be sent to work on the soft fruit section and his big strong hands were no good with delicate soft things. And then he'd have the squashed produce deducted from his wages. It was a nightmare! Why had Fizz decided to run off anyway? (He'd told Kevin he'd be back by six, so where was he? How worried, she wondered, should she be?)

And then her thoughts were interrupted by a noise from outside.

There was a crash, like someone knocking over a dustbin and falling into a puddle in a heap, and then the shout of a supermarket owner.

'You! What are you doing out there? Boy!'

Let's turn the clock back a few minutes.

Fizzlebert Stump knew he was late. As he ran through the streets between the park, the library and the supermarket (*not* following Dr Surprise's short cut) he muttered under his breath, 'Faster, Fizz, faster!' But it didn't help.

No nearby church clock tower tolled the six o'clock chimes slowly as they would in a really good book, the sort where the hero gets home just as the last chime strikes and all is well (though sweaty and out of breath). No, six o'clock had long since passed and Fizz was just running, hoping that Kevin had managed to stay out of trouble this long.

As he turned the corner into the supermarket car park he heard a banging and saw Mr Pinkbottle outside the Stumps' caravan.

'Hurry up!' he was shouting.

Fizz thought quickly, his brain spinning and buzzing and whirring in his head, even as his lungs heaved, burnt and wheezed in his chest.

Kevin must be in the caravan.

Pinkbottle looked angry, but not *incredibly*

angry, which must mean that the subterfuge had subterfuged well, so far.

If Fizz could quickly climb in the window and then go out through the door, Mr Pinkbottle would never know he'd been away and Kevin would be able to just go home and everything would be back to 'normal' (the bad new normal, not the good old normal, but still …) and all he'd have to do was wait for Alice to come, later on, and they could put their plan into action.

There was a dustbin just by the side of the caravan, underneath his mum and dad's bed-room window.

Brilliant!

Using all his finest circus skills he climbed up on top of it, but after all that running his legs were a bit wobbly (not having got their breath back (not having lungs of their own (and Fizz, rather selfishly, using the two in his chest all for himself))) and he slipped, fell and crashed to the ground, splashing in a puddle and sending the dustbin flying.

Mr Pinkbottle's face darted round the side of the caravan and his eyes immediately saw the boy lying on the wet ground and his brain immediately recognised exactly which boy it was and his mouth snapped out the words, 'You! What are you doing out there? Boy! Oh ... You push me too far. Out of the kindness of my too-big heart I allow you five minutes for a sandwich and you sneak off into the dark breaking *other people's dustbins*.' He paused to wipe some foam and froth from the side of his froth-foaming lips. 'Oh, you little vandal, you vex me greatly.'

'Sorry, Mr Pinkbottle,' said Fizz, climbing slowly to his feet.

'Sorry? Sorry!? Look at your uniform, you wretch. Look at it!'

Fizz looked down. He was muddy and wet and covered in grit and bin juice. A leaf of limp lettuce dangled from his shoulder.

'Sorry, Mr Pinkbottle,' he repeated, feeling as limp as the aforementioned lettuce leaf.

Mr Pinkbottle made a noise like an unimpressed panda and turned his back on the boy.

'Everything I do, Stump, is for your own good. All my *kindness*. All my *generosity*. I take you in, give you work. I give you food off my very plate … and this … this is how you repay me.'

He shook his head.

'What's going on out here?' asked Mrs

Stump, coming round the corner of the caravan.

'Ingratitude,' said Mr Pinkbottle.

'Fizz?' said his mum. 'What are you doing there?'

'It's obvious,' hissed Mr Pinkbottle, looking at where Fizz was standing, at the spilt dustbin and at the caravan window above. 'He was running away … again.'

'I'm sure that's not true,' Mrs Stump said. 'He probably … um … fell out the window, while getting changed.' (She winked at Fizz as she said it.)

'That's it,' said Fizz.

There was a quiet *donk!* at the window and everyone looked up to see a boy's face looking out at them. A boy's face that quickly vanished.

'Who's that?' snapped Mr Pinkbottle, looking from one face to another.

Fizz's heart thumped. Oh no!

Mr Pinkbottle lurched round the caravan, round to the side with the door, and Fizz heard the thwack of a clipboard meeting boy-skull and the banging succession of thuds as a body fell down several steps.

He ran, with his mum, to see what had happened.

They found Mr Pinkbottle stood over the shape of a crumpled Kevin (still half in the gorilla suit (the bottom half)) lying in a puddle at the foot of the caravan's steps.

'I seem to have found a burglar,' Mr Pinkbottle said. 'He was in your caravan, Mrs Stump. You really ought to be more careful.'

'Kevin,' said Fizz, kneeling down at his side. 'You OK?'

The boy was groaning and rubbing the side of his head, but seemed otherwise unharmed.

'Oh?' said Mr Pinkbottle, acting surprised. 'You know this little miscreant, do you? He seems to have stolen half of my charity costume. Only the lowest sort of pond-life steals from a charity, Young Master Stump. You really should keep better company than this.'

He tutted and shook his head.

Kevin looked at Fizz and Fizz looked at Kevin and Fizz's mum looked at Kevin and Kevin looked at Fizz's mum and Fizz looked at Fizz's mum too and then Fizz's mum looked at

Fizz, at which point everyone had looked at everyone else and so they all looked at the floor instead.

It was ten minutes later and they were sat on boxes of tinned peas and baked beans and baked beans with little sausages and tinned green beans and pies and potatoes and chicken soup and tomato soup and mushroom and chicken soup and … Well, basically on boxes of *tinned food, various*.

They were in one of the supermarket's storerooms and Mr Pinkbottle had locked the door on them.

'It's not fair,' said Fizz.

A single lightbulb flickered yellowly above them.

'I don't know what you were playing at,' his mum said. Not angrily. Tiredly.

She meant running off and swapping places with Kevin and all that.

Mr Pinkbottle hadn't taken it very well, not that Fizz had tried to explain to him what he'd been up to. (That's always a stupid idea, telling your arch-enemy all your plans (it's where most villains fall down, for example: when they've captured the hero, instead of just dropping them straight in the shark tank, they spend so long boasting about their plans for world domination that the hero has time to escape from his or her ropes and *THWACK!* a sudden uppercut puts pay to the fiend and her or his plans).)

Mr Pinkbottle had grumbled about betrayal and trust and had said he was going to ring the police about the trespassing impostering burglar (Kevin) and that he'd think up a new suitable punishment for Fizz, who'd tried running away two days in a row (even though on both days he'd only been caught when he came home again, so it wasn't *really* running away). And at that point Fizz's mum had said, 'I don't think you're being entirely fair, Mr Pinkbottle,' and Fizz had felt his muscles bubbling in his arms as if he wanted to punch the man (but he didn't).

Mr Pinkbottle didn't like being interrupted or being contradicted or being fifty-seven (although there was nothing much he could do about that last one), and so he locked them all in the storeroom, out of the way.

Fizz had considered resisting, fighting his way free and making a run for it, going and finding his dad or Dr Surprise or *someone* who'd be able to help, but he didn't. Not because he was afraid, but because he didn't think it would do much good. It wouldn't help with their plan and it wouldn't make things easier for his mum or Kevin if (a) he managed to run off or (b) he didn't. And he knew he couldn't rely on (c) getting help, because everyone was afraid of Mr Pinkbottle and they all did as he said, because he was the boss. (Fizz didn't much like having a boss. Few people do.)

And so they were stuck in the storeroom. It had no windows to get out of and the door was heavy and bolted on the other side.

'At least we're not going to starve,' said Kevin.

He pulled a chocolate bar out of one of the boxes and offered it to Mrs Stump.

'Thank you,' she said, 'but it's not ours. We can't eat this food.'

'Mum,' Fizz said. 'Don't be silly. We should eat it all. That would serve Pinkbottle right.'

'*Mister* Pinkbottle,' she corrected.

'Oh, Pinkbottle, Winkdottle, Thinkspottle,' said Fizz. 'I don't care about his stupid name and I don't care about being polite. This is all wrong, Mum,' he said, 'don't you see? There's something peculiar going on and we think we know what it is. Sort of.'

'We?'

He told them about what Alice had said, her ideas about their blackmailed Ringmaster. And he told them the plan they'd made to find the evidence.

'But now I'm stuck in here, I don't know how we're going to do it,' he said.

'We're gonna have to wait,' said Kevin, looking at his watch.

Fizz's mum looked like she'd understood everything Fizz had told her, but that she wasn't entirely convinced by it.

'I don't know,' she said. 'That all sounds a bit far-fetched, Fizz. The Ringmaster *had* to sell the circus to Mr Pinkbottle, you know that, because … Well, for *reasons*.' She paused for a moment as if wondering what those *reasons* actually were. The Ringmaster had never quite got round to explaining properly. After a moment she waved the pause away with her hand and went on talking. 'And besides, it's not the Ringmaster's fault that it turned out Mr Pinkbottle had different ideas for the circus than he'd expected. Not his fault at all.' Fizz couldn't help but think she gave the Ringmaster a little too much benefit of the doubt. 'I suggest we just sit here quietly,' she said, 'and wait for Mr Pinkbottle to open the door, which I'm sure he'll do any moment now. Now he's had a few minutes to calm down and think about it. He's very emotional, that's all.'

Nevertheless, she took the chocolate bar and broke it into three bits.

'Just to keep our strength up,' she said.

Hours went by.

'Any minute now,' said Mrs Stump.

And another couple of hours went by.

Fizz woke up.

The little yellow lightbulb still flickered and buzzed above them.

His mum was snoring gently on top of a big box of powdered milk.

Kevin was looking at him.

'What time is it?' Fizz whispered.

'Almost eleven,' Kevin said, looking at his watch. 'Do you think he's going to open the door soon? I reckon my mum and dad'll be worried by now. They'll probably have phoned the police again.'

'I think,' Fizz said, 'that we're in here for the night.'

'Oh,' said Kevin. It looked like the thrill of adventure he'd felt earlier had long since worn off. He looked like he had when Fizz had first met him, locked up in the Stinkthrottle's kitchen. He looked tired and sad and small again.

'Oh come on,' Fizz said. 'Cheer up Kevin.

It's not as bad as all that. We got out of trouble before, didn't we? We're gonna do it again, I'm sure.'

Kevin said nothing.

The lightbulb flickered, buzzed and went out with a pop.

The darkness was total and time continued to pass by.

And that's where we'll leave them. It's too dark to see what's happening, so there's no point me trying to explain what's going on, after all you wouldn't be able to read the words, unless they were illuminated and we don't have the budget for that sort of stuff.

Instead, we'll just have to move on to the next chapter and see if that's any brighter.

CHAPTER NINE

In which a girl runs away from the cicrus and in which some horrible tea is drunk

Alice Crudge exited the ring to a fairly decent ripple of applause. (The sixteen people watching had quite enjoyed her act (in which she lifted up a variety of heavy things, finishing up by juggling three lead balloons (which were painted to look colourful and sparkly and which a member of the audience had tried lifting first, to prove they weren't filled with helium or something)).)

She passed her father in the backstage area. He was still dressed as a cloud and was still grumbling as he walked into the ring to take part in the cicrus's big finale, a live zeppelin race. He gave her a half-smile. (He disapproved of her act, mainly because the famous Crudge strength had skipped a generation, leaving him without muscles of any special note.)

During the show she'd almost dropped her twirling dumbbells because she'd been thinking about Fizz and about what they'd be doing later on. They had a plan to unfold and a villain to uncover. That was more exciting than slightly impressing sixteen people in an audience.

She watched the finale through the curtains and bounced out at the end to take the big group bow with the rest of the cicrus. She smiled like she meant it, but her mind wasn't on showbiz. She was trying to remember where she'd put her black jumper. Was it in the laundry basket, or was it down the back of her fold-up bed?

After the show she ate supper with her dad, who was silent and yet still managed to grumble. They had beans on toast that she burnt, her mind being more concerned about trying to remember where her black gloves were.

After an hour or so her dad went to bed, saying a mumbled, 'Goodnight,' and leaving her alone in the kitchen-cum-bedroom.

She washed up the dishes and unfolded her bed.

There was her black jumper, just where she'd left it.

She brushed her teeth and washed her hands and face. Then she got changed, but not ready for bed like normal. Instead she put on her black jumper and black jeans. She cut two eyeholes in her dad's spare eye mask, instantly changing it from a sleeping mask to a burgling mask, and slipped it on to her face. She laced up her comfiest trainers and pulled a black woolly hat over her ears, picked up a pair of gloves (they were inside the hat) and slipped out the caravan door, shutting it slowly and silently behind her.

She crept out of the circle of cicrus caravans and through the park, past the duck pond, between trees and towards the exit.

She followed the directions Fizzlebert had

given her, noting the library as she passed it by, and turned on to the street heading towards Pinkbottle's Supermarket.

It was late and the streets were mostly empty. The streetlights were those ones that shone orange in the puddles, dim and autumnal.

She dodged out of the way of a long roadside

puddle that a passing bus attempted to share with her, only to tread on a loose paving stone that squirted dirty cold water straight up her trouser leg.

But even this didn't dampen her spirits: she was on an adventure *and* was going to help a pal out of a sticky corner. What could be better? (Doing it in the dry maybe, but still . . .)

Soon she was at the supermarket.

She looked at her watch.

It was eleven o'clock. At night.

'Zero hour,' she said to herself, meaning, 'Synchronise watches, we're going in,' meaning, 'This is the time that Fizz said we'd meet and begin unfolding our plan.'

Except Fizz wasn't there.

She was looking into the private car park

at the back of the shop and she knew it was the right place because she could see the tiny gaggle of caravans and the big doors where lorries unloaded their goods.

Fizz was supposed to come and meet her and they'd go into the supermarket together.

(He'd said that the woman, Mrs Leavings, might be guarding the shop's back door. If she was then Alice was to cause a diversion by making a noise in the street (she was good at that sort of thing) and he'd slip in by himself, but since the woman wasn't there Alice didn't distract her, not needing to.)

But where was Fizz?

After waiting a few minutes in the shadows, until she was sure there was no one else about, she tiptoed over to Fizz's caravan.

There was still a light on so she knocked on the door.

There was a clattering from inside and it sounded like someone had fallen over and then the door opened and the light that should have spilt from the doorway into the night, dazzling Alice's eyes and making her blink, never came because it was blocked by a huge figure looming darkly above her.

'Hello?' said a voice. 'Is there somebody there?'

Alice gathered her courage, not because she was *scared*, but because she was *starstruck*. She knew who this man was. He was her hero. Her throat felt dry. She coughed, swallowed and spoke.

'Mr Stump,' she said. 'It's me. Alice. Alice

Crudge. I was wondering if Fizzlebert was at home?'

Alice was a stronggirl. She had muscles far beyond the normal person. All her life she had wanted to be a strongperson like her famous grandfather, but her dad (the generation, as I mentioned before, that the great Crudge strength had skipped) had made her do other things, other acts. (She had been an above-average flower arranger when Fizz had first met her, but she'd never told him about the mediocre sandwich-making act she'd done before that, or the quite rubbish soft-toy-juggling one before *that*.)

As a wannabe stronggirl she'd read the British Board of Circuses' Newsletter avidly for news of other strongperson acts, and had memorised everything lifted up by Mr Stump (there'd been a complete list in the New Year special). And so, when they'd met (three-quarters of the way through *Fizzlebert Stump and the Girl Who Lifted Quite Heavy Things*) she'd been shy and embarrassed and had talked too much and had possibly even blushed (they'd then done a show together, but if you've not read that book ignore what I just said, because I don't want to spoil it for you).

And so, meeting him again, for her, was still just as exciting.

'Alice?' said Mr Stump. 'You don't *look* like Alice. Who are you really?'

Alice pulled the mask from her face.

'Alice Crudge! It is you! Oh my!' cried Mr Stump.

(As excited to see Mr Stump as Alice was, he was just as excited to be re-meeting her. Her grandfather, Avuncular Crudge, had been Mr Stump's hero since he was a boy. (Crudge's was the only autograph the young Mr Stump had ever collected.) Since Avuncular Crudge was long retired from the business (he now ran a second-hand antiques shop on the coast), Alice was the

next best thing (and quite possibly the next *better* thing, since she was possibly, and certainly would be by the time she grew up, even *stronger* than her grandfather, and that was what really mattered in strongperson circles: not who you were, but how much you could lift).)

'Come in,' he said, almost stuttering as he stepped back into the caravan.

Alice climbed the steps as best she could, and ventured inside.

'Is Fizz here?' she asked, as Mr Stump clicked the kettle on.

He was wearing a blue stripy nightshirt and nightcap like a character from an old film. (It made Mrs Stump laugh when the cap dangled in front of his face and he liked making her laugh.)

'Fizz? No, him and his mum have gone on holiday.'

'On holiday?' she asked.

This was news to her.

'Yes,' Mr Stump said, taking two mugs from the drying rack by the sink. 'It was a last-minute, spur of the moment thing. You know how it is.'

She didn't.

'I was supposed to be meeting him here,' she said. 'He can't have gone –'

'It was a surprise to me too,' he said, pouring boiling water on to two tea bags. 'I was stacking fruit all evening and when I came back here for my supper, they were gone. Mr Pinkbottle explained it though. Fizz won the "Employee of the Month" prize, three days in Acapulco, and because you can't send a boy on holiday to Acapulco by himself, Gloria went with him.'

Alice thought about this and thought about the things that Fizz had told her.

'Are you sure?' she said.

'Yes,' Mr Stump. 'You definitely can't send a boy to Acapulco by himself. Not at his age.'

'No, I mean are you sure that's where they've gone? On holiday?'

'Yes, of course. Where else could they have gone?' Mr Stump asked, but Alice could tell he wasn't as certain as he was trying to make out.

'But it doesn't make sense, Mr Stump.'

He said nothing for a moment and looked around.

'I did wonder,' he eventually said, 'why

they hadn't taken any clothes with them, but Mr Pinkbottle said it's very hot in Acapulco at this time of year.'

Alice sipped at her tea. It wasn't very nice. She liked tea normally, but this tasted rather like drinking a tortoise.

'Mr Stump,' she said. 'I've got to tell you something.'

And she, even though she'd promised Fizz to keep the secret plan secret, told Mr Stump their secret plan and their secret suspicions about the supermarket and its untrustworthy master.

It took a while for the words she was saying to trickle down into the correct corners of Mr Stump's brain (his brain not being the biggest muscle in his body (not really being a muscle at all, now I think about it, but you know what I mean)). But, eventually, even a brain as powerful as his has to turn around and say, 'Hang on a moment!'

'Hang on a moment!' Mr Stump said, echoing the words of his brain. 'Are you saying the Ringmaster's being *blackmailed*?'

'Exactly,' she said.

She ran through the facts that made that seem the only explanation, again.

'And you think Fizz and Gloria … aren't on holiday?'

'I seriously doubt it,' she said.

'Oh,' he said.

'But where they've really got to … I don't know.'

She swallowed the last of her tea.

'Mr Stump,' she said. 'Fizz or no Fizz,

we've got to go through with this plan. Agreed?'

Mr Stump put his mug down.

'It's horrible, this tea,' he said, before reaching over and shaking her hand. 'Let's do it.'

Chapter Ten's going to be a good one. Better than this one anyway. I mean, what really happened here? Alice Crudge met Mr Stump, again. That's it. That's hardly the most exciting, adventurous chapter ever written, is it? Sorry about that. (Sometimes, however, you need a chapter like this to (a) explain what's going on and (b) fill a bit of space (if I hadn't written this, for example, there'd've been eighteen blank pages between Chapter Eight and Chapter Ten and that would've just looked weird and you'd've thought your book was broken or not all the story had loaded or something).)

So, now … eventually … onwards to adventure!

CHAPTER TEN

In which some burglary-ish activities take place and in which some secrets are discovered and uncovered

Mr Stump moved surprisingly quietly for such a big man.

Alice and he tiptoed across the dark car park up to the back door.

Mrs Leavings was nowhere to be seen tonight.

Alice tried the handle, but the door was locked.

'Do you have a key?' she asked.

Mr Stump nodded and fiddled with the doorknob until it came off in his hand.

'There you go,' he said. 'It's *like* a key.'

On the other side of the door, a second later, the inside handle fell to the concrete floor with a loud rattling metal clatter.

They looked at each other. One of those looks you see in films where a door handle has fallen to the floor in the middle of the night with a rattling metal clatter and the robbers look at each other as if to say, 'Uh-oh.'

And then, suddenly ... nothing happened.

No footsteps came running.

No bright torchlight beam swung into their faces.

No security guard or police officer said, 'You're nicked, sunshine.'

After a moment, suddenly nothing happened again.

When, after a few more moments, nothing happened (suddenly) for a third time, Alice pushed the door with her finger.

It swung gently on its hinges and she stepped inside.

'Which way's Pinkbottle's office?' she asked in a whisper. (Although it was dark inside, and although it didn't seem as if there was anyone around (this was going easier than it had gone when she and Fizz had first imagined the plan) she still felt whispering was the right way to talk.)

Mr Stump explained and Alice headed, carefully, off through the storeroom.

'Hello, hello, hello,' said a voice. 'What's going on here, then?'

A flicker of torchlight played across the ceiling and wall before her, but only a flash, just a sliver, because Mr Stump was still stood in the doorway and whoever had spoken was outside, in the car park.

'Ah,' said Mr Stump, turning to talk to the person.

Alice's heart was beating so loud in her ears she could hardly hear the conversation that began behind her.

Without really thinking, and without turning back or giving up, she slid further into the building.

She knew Mr Stump wouldn't give her away. He'd do his best to keep her safe, to keep her secret. But she'd best be quick. She'd best hurry. Hanging around dawdling would do no one any favours.

And so she went on, deeper into the building.

Mr Stump was dazzled by the light of the torch. He couldn't see who was on the other side of it and he didn't recognise the voice.

He did, however, have a twisted-off door-knob in his hand, which was never a good look in the middle of the night round the back of a shop.

'Ah,' he began, by way of an explanation that explained nothing.

'I think maybe you'd better come with me,' said the voice. (It was a man's voice, belonging to someone quite tall, and possibly with a wiry grey moustache, Mr Stump reckoned, using his eagle-ears and his super-naturally powerful intuition.)

'I can explain,' he said, starting his second unhelpful explanation by not saying anything explanatory.

'Explain what, sir?' asked the voice.

'I live here,' said Mr Stump, pointing towards the caravan with the hand that held the doorknob. 'I mean, I live *there*. I *work* here,' he gestured over his shoulder at the supermarket with the same hand and a bit of metal fell out of the doorknob with a clatter.

'Do you?' said the voice. (It sounded as if it almost didn't believe him.)

The torch was still shining in Mr Stump's eyes.

'Yes,' he said. 'I work for Mr Pinkbottle. I've just been made head of the soft fruit department.' (He had felt proud of this, until Alice had made him see things more clearly.

Now he didn't quite know what to feel, other than cheated and unjustly employed.)

'Soft fruit?' asked the voice, incredulously. 'With those hands?'

'Now, hang on a minute –' began Mr Stump.

'Will you step over here please,' the voice interrupted.

The torch flashed over towards the caravans.

Mr Stump walked over to where it gestured.

The light from the streetlamps lit this bit of car park and finally Mr Stump could see who he was talking to.

It was a short, roundish police officer with no moustache.

(So much for starting up an Eagle-Eared-Man-Can-Describe-You-From-Just-Your-Voice act, thought Mr Stump.)

She said, 'Do you have any ID on you, sir?'

'ID?'

'Yes, to prove who you are.'

'Who I am?'

'Yes, who you are, sir.'

Mr Stump patted his nightshirt.

'Not *on* me,' he said.

'I think I'm going to have to ask you to

accompany me to the station,' the police officer said.

'To the station?' asked Mr Stump. 'Isn't it a bit late? I expect the last train's already gone.' She didn't say anything to that, not because she didn't have a sense of humour, but because it had been a long night already and she had been about to go off duty when she'd noticed this strange man lurking behind the supermarket ... in his nightshirt.

She reached up to her collar and pressed the button on her radio.

'This is PC Singh calling Police Headquarters. PC Singh calling Police Headquarters. Come in Headquarters. Over.'

There was a crackle of static and then a tinny voice said, 'You OK, Ruby?'

'No,' said PC Singh. 'Everything's not

OK. I've apprehended a confused gentleman attempting a forced entry at Pinkbottle's Supermarket. He's refusing to cooperate with my enquiries. I think I may need back-up. Over.'

'Back-up?'

Mr Stump, who was stood two metres away and who was causing no trouble whatsoever, thought back-up probably wasn't necessary and said, 'I don't think you need back-up.'

'All right, Ruby,' came the voice from her radio. 'We're on the way. You hold tight and we'll be there in a few minutes.'

'Cup of tea while we wait?' said Mr Stump, pointing at the caravan.

Indoors, and barely fifty metres to the west of the police constable, Alice Crudge was edging her way, trespassingly, through the behind-the-scenes parts of the supermarket.

There were more storerooms full of stuff than she'd expected.

She'd hardly ever been in a supermarket in her life. Her dad did most of the shopping for them and she had to stay at the cicrus and look after the caravan because he didn't trust Hugh Deeney-Bopper, the cicrus's escapologist. 'He'll be through those locks in seconds,' Mr Crudge would say, 'and then we won't have so much as a teacup left.' (It was an old grudge, made even sillier by the fact that Hugh Deeney-Bopper needed help from audience members every night to *do up* his handcuffs (and more often than not help from the fire brigade to undo them at the end of the act).)

But just because she'd rarely been *inside* a supermarket before didn't mean that Alice Crudge didn't know what a supermarket *was*. She was a stronggirl, not an idiot, after all. She'd read all the *Agnes Black-Whiffle, Girl of Mystery* comics, about a girl who lived in a supermarket by day and had adventures by night. (She hadn't enjoyed them, because it was a rather rubbish old comic, but they were heirlooms her father had handed down to her from her mother the year she left to become a nun and had to give up worldly things, such as rubbish comics. So, she treasured them, even if they weren't very good) and so she knew that a supermarket was a place that sold food and other stuff, which was, let's be clear, more than she needed to know to undertake the sort of mission she was undertaking.

She was worried about Fizzlebert though. Why had he gone missing just as they were about to undertake their great crime? Where could he be now? Was he in danger?

She didn't know, couldn't know. So she carried on with the plan. Maybe, along with the blackmail evidence, she'd find some clue as to where Fizz and his mum were.

Fizz and Kevin were sat in the dark listening to the noise of Fizz's mum snoring.

It was quite a funny snore (she was a clown, after all), and it was keeping them awake. They didn't know, however, that it was keeping them *both* awake because they weren't saying anything because it was dark and Mrs Stump was trying to sleep and they both suspected the other had gone to sleep as well and neither of them wanted to wake anyone up so they were just sitting there in the dark, wide awake and unable to sleep and time went by. Darkly.

Although there was, beyond the snoring, the occasional odd sound of slurping and of what sounded like empty tins rolling on the concrete floor as people shifted around. Neither Fizz nor Kevin (nor Mrs Stump, for that matter) paid them any attention. To pay too close attention to such noises in the middle of the night, in the deep dark, when you've been locked away and everyone else is asleep encourages thoughts of monsters, ghosts and hobgoblins. It was better (for the sanity of one's brain) to write the noises off as the flittering notes of half-dreamt dreams you'd almost slipped into and woken up from. Much better to think that.

And so the dark went on.

Alice tried the handle of the door marked *Manager's Office – Keep Out* but it was locked.

This was the room she wanted.

There was a glass panel in the door and through it, lit by a shaft of orange streetlight from a high window, she could see a desk and rows of filing cabinets. If this wasn't the place a wicked manager would keep secrets hidden then she was a Frenchman. And she wasn't. A Frenchman, that is, although she had once been to the Isle of Wight.

After quickly looking around, to make sure she wasn't being watched, she gave the door handle a sharp tug and, like the one Mr Stump had 'unlocked' outside, it came off in her hand.

She felt a *tiny* bit bad about it, because she didn't like breaking things, but she soon forgot about it as she crept into the office.

Where to look first?

The desk had six drawers. The filing cabinets had twelve drawers (between the four cabinets (which was three each, mathematically speaking)). Then there was a little cupboard and a bookcase against one wall.

And not only that. The desk was heaped with books and files and bits of paper and letters and mugs of stuff that had once been coffee but which were now starting their own civilisations, and there was a computer monitor and a keyboard and a stuffed owl in a bell jar.

The bookcase was the same. It was full of *stuff*. Untidy stuff. Old stuff. Forgotten stuff. *Unnecessary* stuff.

Alice thought it was as if an anteater had picked up all the rubbish that human beings leave lying around in the jungle and in the rainforest and in the Pacific Ocean, sorted out all the least useful bits and bobs and posted them to Mr Pinkbottle with a covering note saying, *Please put this stuff somewhere safe, you never know when it might come in handy*. And he had. And then he'd forgotten about it. And after that he'd added some more things of his own. And then he'd forgotten about them too.

How was she ever going to find what he was using to blackmail the Ringmaster? Among all this stuff? It was impossible.

For the sake of doing *something* she pulled open the nearest of the filing cabinet drawers.

It was stuffed with folders and files, filled with bits of paper.

She lifted one out and opened it.

It was too dark to read the writing, so she carried it back to the door and flicked on the light switch.

There was a buzz, a hum, a shudder and the fluorescent tube overhead popped into life.

She rummaged through the papers in the folder. They looked like contracts or pay slips or something. Nothing to do with the Ringmaster.

She dropped the folder on the floor (which when she looked down she saw was already swimming in papers and old sandwich cartons and crumbs) and went back to the filing cabinet.

At a glance it looked as if the folders in

there would contain the same sort of thing.

This was hopeless. There were hundreds of bits of paper to look at and it would take her forever.

Oh, if only Fizz were here they could do it in half the time. (Half of forever, however, is, unfortunately, still forever.)

Then, as one always does at this point in a story, she heard footsteps out in the corridor.

And they were coming her way.

But it was almost midnight, she thought. *Who on earth is up at this time of night stalking round a supermarket?*

And then she thought, *A burglar! Like me!*

And then she thought, *Oh crumbs! I've turned the light on.*

And then she thought, *Maybe it's Fizz!*

And then she thought, *Still, I ought to hide.*

And then she thought, *Alice, you dummy! Stop thinking and start hiding!*

And then she thought, *OK*.

And then she dived into the space under the desk where the legs of the person sitting at the desk go.

She pulled the chair in behind her.

'Coo-ee!' called a voice. 'Bernard? Are you here?'

Alice didn't know that the voice belonged to Mrs Leavings, because she'd never met or heard the regularly clipboarded lady before.

The footsteps stopped outside the office.

'If you're not here,' Mrs Leavings said, 'then why have you left your light on?'

There was silence for a moment, except it wasn't that silent for Alice because her heart was thumping in her ears.

'And … oh dear …' said Mrs Leavings. 'Your door handle seems to be broken off.'

Alice heard the noise of a toe tapping against a broken door handle on a tiled-but-covered-with-quite-a-lot-of-rubbish floor.

'I wish you'd tidy up sometime, my dear,' the voice went on, talking to the absent 'Bernard' (which Alice assumed, correctly, was Mr Pinkbottle's first name (his parents had wanted one of those mountain rescue dogs with the little brandy barrel round their neck, but had had to make do with a son (and since calling a child 'Saint *something*' is a bit weird, they'd just settled on plain Bernard).)). 'I can't tell if you've been burgled or not. I suspect not, because a burglary would leave your office tidier than before. Oh, Bernard!

It's the one thing that makes me wonder whether I'm right to love you like I do, secretly, hopelessly, desperately.'

Oh gosh, Alice thought. *I do hope she stops talking soon, before she embarrasses one of us*.

'If someone *has* been in here though,' the woman was talking more quietly, more to herself now than to the imagined supermarket manager, 'they'll have gone for your photographs, won't they? Second drawer down on the left-hand side of your desk. I'd best just check they're still there. Just for safe keeping, you know.'

Footsteps, tiptoeing through the accumulated detritus on the floor, stepped closer to Alice, closer to the desk, closer to finding her …

And then another voice yelled in the night.

'Mrs Leavings! Mrs Leavings!'

It was a man's voice. Out in the passage. Further away, but coming nearer.

The footsteps in the room stopped.

'Bernard?'

'Mrs Leavings,' snapped Mr Pinkbottle as he stopped running. 'The police are here! They're out the back. They've got that idiot Stump man and are asking him questions. What the flip's going on, Mrs Leavings?'

'I don't know,' she said.

'And what are you doing in my office?' Mr Pinkbottle shouted, not entirely kindly. (Alice didn't like him, simply because of the way he spoke to Mrs Leavings, never mind all the things that Fizz had told her.) 'I've told you before to get out! It's *my* office.'

'But . . .' said Mrs Leavings, trailing off.

'You need to get out there and deal with the coppers. What do I pay you for? Go and use your *person skills* to make them go away. We don't need them nosing around. Always causing trouble, their sort. I don't like them. Not one bit.'

Mrs Leavings left, followed up the corridor by Mr Pinkbottle, and Alice was on her own again.

All was quiet.

She thought about what she'd just heard.

So, it was the *police* who'd shone the torch at Mr Stump, was it? They'd be useful. If Alice could find the evidence, they were just the people she should show it to. Except, of course, for the fact that she was *trespassing* inside a supermarket at night, rummaging through *private* drawers and *stealing* (hopefully!) a blackmailer's photographs. (Would the police be more angry about *that* or about the blackmail? She didn't know. She could only hope that they'd overlook her *little* crime, when they learnt about the *bigger* one … and when they learnt that Fizzlebert and his mum were missing. (Surely Mr Stump will have told them that already?))

She scooted out from her hiding place and slid open the second drawer down on the left-hand side of the desk.

There was a folder in there labelled: *Blackmail Photographs: Ringmaster – Do Not Lose!*

She hadn't really expected it to be quite so easy.

She lifted the folder out and felt the photographs slide about inside.

Should she open it?

Should she look?

What could be so embarrassing that it would make a man willing to sell his circus?

Outside Mr Stump was lifting PC Singh up with one hand as she giggled.

Three other police officers stood in a little semicircle clapping.

'What's all the noise? Keep it down. Ken's trying to sleep,' shouted Emerald Sparkles, the ex-circus knife thrower, as she approached across the car park. (Ken was actually the name of her third husband, but fortunately her fifth husband, Levi, was hard of hearing and incredibly polite and never made a fuss when she got confused about which was which and muddled up their names.)

'I was telling these nice people about the circus,' said Mr Stump, juggling PC Singh from one hand to the other. 'Can you believe they've never been to the circus?'

'Really?' asked Emerald, rather incredulously.

(It's important to remember that everyone's different, isn't it? Just because you've done something a hundred times or a thousand times, there's always going to be someone out there who's not even done it once. And there'll be things that they think are perfectly ordinary that seem amazing to you, simply because we're all different people with different sets of experiences behind us. (If you learn nothing else from this book, I hope you learn that. (Or how to peel a banana using only your toes, but, to be honest, I'd be surprised (although dreadfully impressed) if *that* was what you took away at the end.)))

You're probably wondering how it is Mr Stump went from being nearly arrested on looking awfully suspicious in his nightshirt by a police officer with back-up on the way, to doing a strongman act at almost midnight in a supermarket car park to an eager audience of coppers.

Well, it went something like this:

(1) While waiting for back-up to arrive Mr Stump put the kettle on and made PC Singh a horrible cup of tea.

(2) On tasting how horrible the tea was she insisted on showing him how to make a nice cup of tea (it's all about the angle at which the teabag and the water intersect).

(3) To do this she went in the caravan and in the process of boiling the kettle (with fresh water (nothing's worse than *re*boiled water for good tea)) she spotted a circus poster on the wall.

(4) She asked Mr Stump about the poster and he explained it was for the circus he used to work in.

(5) She said, 'I've never been to a circus.'

(6) He said, 'What?' and (7) proceeded to tell her all about it.

(8) She changed her opinion about Mr Stump, concluding that (a) he *did* live in the caravan as he'd said, (b) he was in his *nightshirt* because it was almost *midnight* and (c) the way his moustache *twitched* when he was excitedly talking was quite funny in a *cute* way.

And so (9) by the time back-up arrived he was already showing her various heavy things that he could pick up.

It was as Emerald Sparkles went back to her caravan to get her knives (in order to show the police officers some different circus skills to just *lifting things up* (which she, privately, thought wasn't *all that*)) that a commotion was heard coming from the broken door into the supermarket.

Everyone turned to look.

But what they saw won't be revealed until the next chapter.

Dum!-Dum!-Duumm!

(Those, in case you're unsure, are some dramatic chords, implying suspense. I thought I'd put them there because I realised we've not had a lot of dramatic music in this book (a common failing in books, I find) and I thought it was about time for some more.)

CHAPTER ELEVEN

In which some photographs flutter and in which some custard is eaten

'What's going on out here?' said Mrs Leavings, as she burst from the back door into the car park.

She straightened her hair as she said it, and tucked her clipboard under her arm.

Despite the evident hurry, and the time of night, to those who turned to look at her she seemed quite calm.

'It's very late,' she went on, 'and people ought to be sleeping. They've got early mornings, after all, being working people.'

Mr Stump lowered PC Singh to the ground.

'Sorry,' he said.

(Secretly he was worried. He'd been both stalling for time and causing a distraction with all the tea-making and circus tricks. He knew, you remember, that Alice was somewhere inside the supermarket. He hadn't wanted the police to go nosing around in there (it would be bad if they caught her before she'd found the evidence (if it existed)). And he hadn't expected more of them to turn up. But now he was stuck with them. And on top of everything, Mrs Leavings had emerged from the shop, the shop where Alice was.

Had she been found? Had she been caught? Who was exactly in danger from whom?)

'And you are?' asked one of the other police officers, a tall gangly man who wore a pair of what looked like glasses-with-a-false-nose-attached-to-them, but which weren't.

'I'm Marjorie Leavings, deputy manager of this supermarket, and I'd much appreciate it if you'd all move along now and allow my staff some sleep.'

Even as she said this several of the other caravan doors opened and ex-circus faces peered out, woken by the night-time noises and fearful of missing out on some excitement. (Especially since their lives had become so dull recently.)

'Well, Mrs Leavings, my colleague here, PC Singh, was walking in a northerly direction, not so very long ago, when she noticed this gentleman lurking by your back door.' He pointed at Mr Stump. 'Upon investigating the situation it has come to our attention that he is not in fact a burglar, but merely a curious and concerned strongman.'

Mrs Leavings pointed at Mr Stump with her clipboard. 'I know who he is, officer. Thank you. And he ought to be in bed.'

The policeman raised his finger as if to say *I've not finished yet*.

PC Singh took up the story. 'Although I believe Mr Stump innocent of any wrong-doing, I must inform you that there has been some damage done to your back door there. The handle seems to have come off. I believe Mr Stump, however, scared off any intruders you may have had before they intruded.'

'I heard a noise,' Mr Stump improvised. 'And someone ran off when I came out the caravan. That's right.'

'Did they indeed?' said Mrs Leavings coldly. Perhaps she was thinking about the broken handle she'd seen on Mr Pinkbottle's office. She had worrying suspicions growing inside her.

'What's happening?' asked Percy Late, tugging his dressing gown around him.

'Why are there police here?' asked Miss Tremble.

Flopples growled in Dr Surprise's arms.

Mrs Leavings looked around at the little crowd that had gathered.

She tapped her clipboard with a finger and said, 'Everyone! Back to bed. It's late and you're all on earlies.'

'I think,' said the policeman with the nose and glasses, 'that maybe we should just check inside. Just in case a burglar *did* manage to slip in while Mr Stump was getting his slippers on. It's best to be on the safe side.'

He pulled a torch from a pocket and switched it on.

'That's not necessary,' hissed Mrs Leavings. 'I've just come from inside and there was nothing amiss.' (She wanted to get rid of the coppers so she could deal with this herself.)

The word 'amiss' made a small bubble pop in Mr Stump's head.

'Missing!' he spluttered. 'I think Fizz and Gloria are missing!'

'What's this?' asked PC Singh. 'Why didn't you say –'

‘I thought they’d gone on holiday?’ said William Edgebottom, who had joined the crowd. He was holding a potato up so it could see over Madame Plume de Matant’s hat. ‘Employee of the Month and all that? Sorry to interrupt, madam policeman.’ He nodded at PC Singh.

‘That’s right,’ said Mrs Leavings firmly. ‘They’re on holiday. A surprise holiday. A prize holiday.’

The policeman took his glasses off and rubbed the bridge of his nose (which is how everyone knew it wasn’t attached to the glasses and was instead attached to his face, like a normal nose).

‘Can someone explain what’s going on? Do we have another missing person case here or not?’

'*Another?*' asked Percy Late.

'Er, yes. My colleagues are out looking for a lad who's not home from school yet. Second time he's gone off this year. Last time he got himself kidnapped by old folk. Inspector Buckley's doing a door-to-door of sheltered accommodation right now.'

'That rings a bell,' said Mr Stump. 'Is he called ... oh, what was Fizz's friend called?'

He slapped his head to try to get the memories to line up right and knocked himself over.

'Well, I've not seen any stray lost boys here ... it's a supermarket, not a dogs' home, after all ... so I'm going to have to ask you to take your enquiries elsewhere now. Thank you very much,' Mrs Leavings said.

She indicated the gate out of the car park.

'And you lot, back to bed.'

'Kevin!' squeaked Dr Surprise suddenly. 'His name was Kevin, wasn't it?'

'Yes,' declared Captain Fox-Dingle, sticking his head out his caravan window. 'Did trick. Head. Lion. Et cetera.'

'That's right,' said Mr Stump, climbing to his feet. 'Kevin came to the circus and he put his head in the lion's mouth. He did Fizz's trick with him.'

Inside the building, winding the clock back a few minutes so we can re-join her when and where we left her, we see Alice crouched by the desk, clutching the envelope of blackmailable photographs.

She hadn't opened it. She was curious, of course, but it didn't feel right to just open it.

That was Fizz's job, surely? Or even the Ringmaster's, maybe. It wasn't her circus, after all, she was just doing a favour for a friend.

But she hadn't moved either (and because she hadn't moved for so long, hiding away, one of her legs (the right one) had gone numb), she hadn't yet made a run for the door and back out to the car park.

And there was a good reason for that.

And I'm about to tell you what it was.

She'd heard something.

As she'd slid the drawer shut, while pondering what to do, footsteps that had been running away had returned up the corridor outside.

She heard muttering, like someone talking to themselves under their breath, and it was coming closer.

She reckoned it must be the supermarket owner, this Pinkbottle bloke. He'd come back for some reason.

A moment later she discovered the reason. It was a simple reason. An obvious reason.

Mr Pinkbottle had come back in order to help *save the planet*.

That is to say: he reached in and switched off the office light.

A rectangle of floor remained lit by the light that was on in the corridor. His shadow was a dark shape in the middle of the rectangle for a moment, and then it vanished.

He had begun to walk away again.

And then the light in the corridor went out too.

In the dark Alice stretched a leg (the one that had become numb) and, because she couldn't see what junk there was on the floor, she knocked over a *thing*. (Had she been able to see she would have seen it was a pretend can of a popular soft drink that, when it had batteries in it and was switched on, would dance in time with loud music.)

It went *clatter*.

The footsteps stopped, turned around, returned.

The corridor light flicked back on.

The rectangle of floor to Alice's side, stretching across the accumulated rubbish, lit up again.

'What was that?' snapped Mr Pinkbottle. 'Who's there?'

Things crunched underfoot as he made his way into the rubbish-strewn office.

'I can hear you breathing,' he hissed.

Alice stopped breathing.

'You're in deep trouble, you know,' he said. 'Come out now. Come out where I can see you before it gets deeper.'

Alice could see the man's shadow creeping across the floor.

She picked up a button (what was that doing on the floor?) and chucked it over the desk.

'Huh?' said the man, as he heard it ping off something and tinkle to the floor.

(She saw his head turn in the shadow, and he moved, just a step or two, over towards the corner where the button had landed.)

Alice grabbed her opportunity. This was it!

Holding the envelope in her teeth, she pushed with both hands on the underside of the desk, heaving it upwards, using her legs as levers and her arms as pistons.

The table rose a foot, two feet, into the air, and crashed down in front of her, knocking the man off his feet under a flood of *stuff*.

She jumped up and ran for the door.

(Her numb leg was all pins-and-needles-y and really hurt and she wobbled, banging into the doorframe, but then she was in the corridor and Mr Pinkbottle was still on the ground in a sputtering heap.)

She ran back the way she'd come, trying to ignore the noises from the room behind her and the pain in her leg.

She hurtled down the corridor, past doors and round corners and through open spaces piled high with packets of breakfast cereal.

Was this really the way she'd come?

Or had it been *that* way?

It was so hard to know in the dark.

She stood at the junction of two corridors trying to get her bearings, breathing hard and rubbing life back into her tingling leg.

She was scared, her heart was thumping, her lungs ached, and she was up way past her bedtime. She thought to herself, *You know what? This is brilliant!* Better than being in the cicrus, anyway. Maybe she'd become a super-strong spy when she grew up.

There were footsteps behind her, running towards her, and then she saw the glowing green light spelling the word 'Exit' at the end of one of the corridors and she lurched into action.

'Get back here,' yelled Mr Pinkbottle. 'Stop! Thief!'

He was dogged in his pursuit. Panting and yelping.

Alice ran and skidded as her foot landed in a slick of slippery stuff.

Wobbling and unsteady, sliding on one foot like a skateboarder who's jumped off her skateboard only to land on an icy puddle, she hurtled forward, but then, with the elegance and skill of a true circus (*not* cicrus) performer, she regained her footing and ran for the door.

Behind her the short supermarket manager wasn't so lucky, skilful or elegant, and he slipped in whatever it was and fell with a splashing, sliding crash to the floor.

She smiled as she heard the crash and then put her fingers in her ears as she heard the language that erupted from the fallen man.

She burst out through the door like a train out of Hull and every set of eyes in the car park turned to look at her as she missed her footing on the first step and tumbled forward towards the puddled tarmac.

Elsewhere Fizzlebert Stump was still in the dark.

He'd heard running footsteps and muffled swearing outside the door, but he wasn't sure if it was real or if he'd been dreaming.

'What was that?' said Kevin.

Fizz's mum snored gently.

'I think something happened outside,' Fizz said.

'Do you think it's a rescue party?' Kevin asked.

'I don't know,' said Fizz. 'I thought I heard some swearing. I think that might've been Mister Pinkbottle.'

'Oh,' said Kevin. It was a disappointed 'Oh' because, he thought, quite rightly, it was unlikely the man who'd locked them in would be the one to rescue them.

'I'm going to go nearer the door,' Fizz said. 'I'll see if I can hear anything there.'

In the pitch darkness he climbed down from the box of cans he'd been lying on and put his feet on the floor.

'Ooh,' he said. 'The floor's all slippery.'

'What?' said Kevin.

'I think something's spilt,' said Fizz. 'Something's leaked out. The floor's all squelchy.'

'It wasn't me,' said Kevin.

Now the noises outside had stopped, Fizz found it hard, without being able to see, to know which way it was to the door.

He slid his feet slowly through the gloop on the floor and shuffled with his hands held out in front of him like a zombie with fingers that could sense brains.

Suddenly Kevin shrieked.

There was a clatter as he, and who knew how many cans of who knew what, fell to the floor.

'What is it?' Fizz asked, urgently.

'Something touched me! I felt it touch my face. Cold and horrible.'

Fizz had thought his fingers had touched something, just for a moment, but then it had vanished just as Kevin had screamed.

He put two and two together and explained the answer to his friend.

'Oh,' said Kevin, embarrassed. He paused. 'I'm on the floor, Fizz,' he went on. 'You're right, there's something slippery and cold down here. It's all over the place. And it smells like … Oh, it *tastes* like …'

Mrs Stump carried on snoring, oblivious to the boys' conversation.

Outside, Alice Crudge was falling forward through space, and the envelope she had been carrying was flying upwards through a different bit of space. (Neither of them were the sort of space in *outer* space, which would be quite exciting, don't you think? I just mean, 'through the air'.)

She curled as she fell, and rolled, safely and damply, across the ground before bouncing to her feet and saying, 'Ta-da!' (She hadn't meant to, but sometimes circus instincts take control.)

Above her large glossy snowflakes were fluttering slowly downwards.

'Hello, hello, hello,' said a man who was dressed as a policeman. 'Were you supposed to be in there, little girl?'

'A burglar!' yelped a woman with a clip-board that Alice assumed was Mrs Leavings.

'I'm afraid I'm going to have to ask you some questions,' said the man dressed as a policeman who Alice was beginning to think might actually *be* a policeman, as he stepped forward and placed a big hand on her shoulder.

'Leave her alone,' said Mr Stump, stepping forward and placing an even bigger hand on the policeman's shoulder. 'She's with me. If you're going to arrest her, you'll have to arrest me too.'

There was laughter.

Laughter in the car park.

What's that all about? Alice thought. It didn't seem to be funny to her.

But when she looked the people laughing (Dr Surprise and Miss Tremble, who she'd met before) weren't laughing at her. Instead they were holding in front of them a piece of the large glossy snow, which hadn't been snow at all, but rather blackmail photographs.

'What is it?' she said. 'What's the photograph of?'

'Blackmail,' said a shorter police officer who Alice hadn't met before but who we know to be PC Singh.

She was holding the envelope the photographs had been kept in. She read the words, 'Blackmail photographs: Ringmaster – do not lose!' out loud.

'Yes, it's him all right,' said Dr Surprise. 'Those eyebrows are unmistakeable.'

'Young,' declared Captain Fox-Dingle, peering at the photograph he'd caught.

'Oh, but wasn't he cute?' said Miss Tremble. She looked closer at the picture in the doctor's hand. 'Um … Why's he wearing a crown?'

'Blackmail?' said Mr Stump. 'That's what Fizz thought had happened. He said Mr Pinkbottle had blackmailed the Ringmaster into selling the circus.'

'That's ridiculous,' said Mrs Leavings. 'Utterly ridiculous. Those photographs are private property, and this *girl* has stolen them. Police people – arrest the wretch and retrieve the photographs, before they get damaged.'

'I'm not sure I can do that,' said the policeman with the nose and glasses, lifting his hand off Alice's shoulder. 'These are some very serious accusations here and, our friend, Mr Stump, deserves to be listened to. As does his friend.' (He meant Alice.)

(Mr Stump's plan (even though he hadn't really known it was a plan at the time) of making friends with the police and not being bossy and horrible like Mrs Leavings had paid dividends.)

PC Singh handed the envelope with the incriminating words written on it to her colleague.

The giggling and muttering continued among the gaggle of curious ex-circus folk. They were passing photos back and forth and chuckling.

William Edgebottom covered his potato's eyes so it didn't have to see. (Which wasn't entirely necessary since the eyes of a potato aren't things for looking at other things with, they're simply spots from which a shoot will grow, if the potato is buried and watered.)

Then he chuckled too.

'What's so embarrassing,' Miss Tremble asked, 'about a teenage Ringmaster dressed up like a member of Aldonian royalty? Why is this blackmailable? I don't get it. So, he had floppy hair and spots and went to a fancy dress party. We've all done that. When I was seven my mum dressed me as a trifle and, sure, I'd rather the photos didn't get out, but I wouldn't *sell the circus* because of it.'

'Let's see,' said Alice.

Captain Fox-Dingle handed her the photo he'd caught.

In it the Ringmaster, aged maybe thirteen or fourteen or fifteen, was sat on a hard-looking wooden chair, ornately carved and rather splendid in its own way. On his head was a little golden crown, with red velvet lining and fat gems and in his hands, laid across his lap, was a big white cat. It was wearing a collar almost as jewel-encrusted as the crown, and it looked into the camera with the purest blue eyes Alice had ever seen.

To the side of the chair (she was tempted to use the word 'throne' for some reason) she could see the edge of another chair, taller, bigger, gold-coloured. It was cut off, only a tiny bit of it was in shot, but she could see an elbow resting on the armrest, swathed in velvet and the end of a golden *something* (a stick or rod or … *sceptre*, why did that word spring to mind?) was resting on the arm.

The Ringmaster's face was stern, bored, sad even. It didn't look like the face of a lad at a party. It didn't look like someone who was enjoying themselves very much.

Was the Ringmaster so embarrassed, she wondered, about having been bored at a party thirty or forty years ago that he'd be willing to sell the circus to keep the secret? It was madness. She knew *that* couldn't be the reason. So what was it?

'I think I'd best collect all this stuff up, for safe keeping,' said PC Singh, snatching the photo from between Alice's fingers. 'As *evidence*,' she added.

Dr Surprise coughed quietly and said, 'My friends. A long time ago the Ringmaster entrusted me with a secret, which I have faithfully kept, but now, I think, you deserve to know the truth.'

As he said these words, and as PC Singh was extracting the photos from the grips of the rest of the crowd a noise of inchoate fury thundered from the supermarket's back door, interrupting the doctor's explanation.

All eyes turned to see a short, pointy-faced man with sideburns and a sheen of yellow slime dripping from all over, burst out into the night.

'AAArrrgggHhhhGhH!' he yelled.

(He seemed to be a bit miffed about something.)

'Calm down there, Wet Pants,' said the policeman with the big nose.

Mr Pinkbottle stopped and dripped and blustered and rubbed his eyes and dripped a bit more and stared at the policeman.

'Flinch,' he said. 'What are *you* doing here?'

'*Sergeant* Flinch, to you ... *sir*,' said the policeman.

Mr Stump looked from one to the other.

'Do you know this man?' he said (asking the policeman if he knew the supermarket man).

'What?' said the policeman. 'Do I know *Bernie Wet Pants*?' He coughed, went, 'Ahem,' and straightened himself up to speak sensibly like a policeman ought. 'I mean "Do I know Mr Bernard Pinkbottle?" Oh yes, I should say so. We were at school together. A long time ago now. Years back, but I never forget a face. Or name. Except for … oh … *you-know*.' His face went all wistful and sad for a few seconds as he tried to think. '*What's-her-name* … I just can't remember what *she* looks like. But other than that, I never forget.'

'That's an unusual surname,' said Dr

Surprise, stroking a growling Flopples in his arms. '"*Wet Pants*". No wonder he changed it to "Pinkbottle".'

'Oh, I shouldn't call him that. Not when I'm on duty,' Sergeant Flinch said. 'It's just that I've never forgotten the smell on the coach coming back from the circus. No one who was on that trip's forgotten it. We were, what? Seven? Eight, maybe? Getting on for half a century ago, now. And at every school reunion people still ask me if I know what Bernie Wet Pants is up to. Nicknames have a habit of sticking, sometimes.'

Mr Pinkbottle was fuming and bubbling. 'I hate you, Flinch. I hate everyone in Ocelot Class. Even Miss Whitman. Even she pointed and called me by *that name*.'

'You're misremembering, Mr Pinkbottle,'

said Sergeant Flinch. '*She* called you "Bernard Soggy Socks". Marvellous way with words, that woman. Taught me so much.'

'One day … One day I'll have my revenge on her, too.'

'It was a school trip to the circus, you see,' Sergeant Flinch began to explain. 'Young Master Pinkbottle was surprised by a human cannonball –'

'It was a *very* loud bang,' snapped Pinkbottle.

'– and found he'd had a little accident in his …'

The sergeant left the end of the sentence hanging in the air.

'It left him with an irrational fear of circuses and circus performers –'

'Not *irrational*,' interrupted Mrs Leavings.

'All those *sequins* ... they're a proper health and safety nightmare. Very easy to choke on.' She shuddered. 'Not irrational at all.'

The sergeant ignored her and continued, 'This is actually the third time he's blackmailed a Ringmaster into selling his circus.'

'Blackmail?' shouted Mr Pinkbottle. 'I've not ...'

He stopped talking when PC Singh held up the envelope of photos.

'Oh,' he said.

'After the last time he promised us he'd not do it again,' the sergeant said. 'But it just goes to show, once a Wet Pants, always a Wet Pants.'

(This doesn't, strictly speaking, make sense as an argument, and you could make a certain case to suggest that had Sergeant Flinch (pre-police career) and his classmates (and teacher) not taken the mickey out of young Bernard all those years ago he might have grown up to be a nice man … But you never know. Bullying is a bad thing, yes, but Mr Pinkbottle might've still become an unpleasant man for all sorts of other reasons. It's hard to say for certain.)

Mr Stump looked at the supermarket manager and at what was dripping off him today. It wasn't what had dripped down all those years before, he thought (although that too had been yellow).

'Is that custard?' he said.

Pinkbottle gave him a look, and realised that the game was finally all up. His shoulders sagged as if he was giving up and giving in and then, like a human cannonball from a cannon, he was off running.

'What have you done with Gloria!' shouted Mr Stump.

'Catch that man!' shouted Sergeant Flinch.

'Darling!' shouted Mrs Leavings, reaching out for the fleeing villain. 'I don't care about the wet pants. Come back!'

Ftang! Ftang! Ftang!

Mr Pinkbottle suddenly stopped running.

He'd been passing the Stumps' caravan, but now he was dangling.

His suit seemed to be attached to the caravan at three points, as if it had been stapled there and he'd fallen or slipped and was waiting, suspended, for someone to come and unpin him.

'No need to thank me,' said Emerald Sparkles, circus knife thrower, blowing on her fingertips.

'Ah,' said Dr Surprise, 'but we *should* thank Flopples.'

They turned to see Mrs Leavings, who had just darted in the opposite direction, lying on her front, pinned to a puddle by a growling, sharp-toothed, nose-twitching rabbit. Oh, of course she was wriggling and trying to escape, but the rabbit had a firm grip on her collar and a wicked gleam in her eye.

Fizzlebert Stump, and Kevin, had heard none of what had just happened outside, but a minute later the door to the storeroom was ripped off its hinges and light flooded in on them for the first time in ages.

They blinked and rubbed their eyes and looked around them.

Mrs Stump was still snoring.

'Oh, Mum,' Fizz said, quietly so as to not wake her up. 'You've been sleep-eating again.'

All around her were open packets and cans of custard and there was a smear of yellow loveliness around her lips.

The custard had dripped all over the floor.

So much so that custard had even leaked under the door and out into the corridor.

Fizz's dad was in the doorway, and so was Alice.

'There you are,' she said and punched him on the arm. 'Lazing around while me and your dad do all the work.'

When Fizz got up he introduced her to Kevin.

'Kevin!' said Mr Stump. 'I thought you were missing. The policeman said … But what are you doing here?'

'It's a long story,' said Fizz. 'What's the ending look like?'

Out in the car park Kevin went over to PC Singh and said, 'Excuse me. I think you might be looking for me.' He explained who he was.

PC Singh radioed back to base and base telephoned his parents and his parents got dressed and went round to Mr Furbelow next door and asked if he'd drive them to the supermarket. (Their own car was in the garage for a service.) Mr Furbelow, still in his pyjamas, began the search for his car keys, which he'd definitely had in the kitchen before dinner, but were now …

Eventually Kevin's mum and dad walked across town to the supermarket (arriving just as Mr Furbelow turned up and kindly offered to give them all a lift home).

They were a *little* surprised to see Fizzlebert and the other circus folk there, but not *too* surprised.

'Do we get more free tickets?' they asked.

But there wasn't any real reply to that, because this time Fizz didn't have a circus to invite them to.

And that's almost the end. All that's left is tying up the loose threads and a glimpse into the future, and we'll do that in a little dangling final chapter, right after the break.

CHAPTER TWELVE

In which loose threads are tied up and in which the future is glimpsed

After the police had hauled Mr Pinkbottle and Mrs Leavings away for further questioning about the kidnapping and locking away of Kevin and Fizz and his mum, and other questions about the envelope of photos labelled *Blackmail*, the Ringmaster emerged from his caravan.

He yawned and stretched as he climbed

down the steps.

(Mr Stump had explained what had been in the blackmail envelope to Fizz and his mum while they were waiting for Kevin to be picked up.)

'Why's everyone up?' the Ringmaster asked. 'What's been going on? It's awfully late.'

Once the giggling had died down (once you've seen a photograph of someone you know as a grown-up when they were a spotty, floppy-haired teenager, it's hard to forget that image, however serious you try to be) and after a moment of silence in which no one could quite bring themselves to look him in the eye, Fizz spoke up.

'Ringmaster,' he said. 'You sold the circus. You sold our home, our family, our acts. Because of a few embarrassing photographs? Well, it's over now. We can take back our contracts and leave this supermarket. We can get back on the road and get on with what we're supposed to be doing. We're not *normal* people, we're not meant for *normal* lives, for *normal* jobs like this.' He pointed at the supermarket. 'Supermarkets are important, they put cornflakes in people's bowls and milk in their tea, but we … we put smiles on people's faces and sawdust in their … I mean, *stardust* in their eyes. That's what we're meant to be doing. But … but you sold it all. You gave it away. I'm … I'm sorry …'

Mr Stump put his hand on his son's shoulder and pulled him into a hug.

'It's OK, Fizz,' he said. 'We'll be OK now. Thanks to you.'

'And to Alice,' added Dr Surprise.

Alice murmured something, not wanting to show off.

The Ringmaster hung his head low. He'd been found out. Caught out. He'd lost that thing that all Ringmasters need: respect.

'I was …' he began. 'He had …'

'Your Highness,' said Dr Surprise.

The Ringmaster looked up sharply. His face fell. *They knew his secret*.

'What do you mean?' Miss Tremble said. '*Your Highness?*'

The Ringmaster looked at Dr Surprise, then at Miss Tremble.

'I *was* about to explain,' the doctor said. 'But things got a bit hectic and the moment had passed. They've seen the photos, though.'

The Ringmaster sighed.

‘If it came out,’ he said. ‘If they found out where I was, I’d have to go back. I was born Prince Rudolf Flanderfuff, only son of my parents, the King and Queen of Aldonia.’

‘Ooh la la,’ said Madame Plume de Matant.

‘Gosh,’ said Alice, quietly.

‘I hated it. I hated being a prince. I hated all the expectations, all the paperwork, all the endless, tedious cocktail parties and bowling alley opening ceremonies. Aldonia's not a big country, but it has a lot of bowling alleys that need opening. A lot of ribbons to cut, and that was my responsibility. My father, the King, had even more responsibility, more paperwork, and more people coming and asking to rub his moustache for luck. I couldn't face ending up like that, so when I was seventeen I ran away and joined the circus. I never looked back. I love the circus, it's my world now … you're my friends. I only ever wanted to …'

'Ringmaster,' said Fizz, speaking up when the Ringmaster's words ran out of steam. 'I don't know anything about being a prince or being a king or anything like that. But what I do know is that you let us down. You didn't trust us. You never spoke up. We were your friends. Your family. You should've trusted us.'

'But I stayed,' said the Ringmaster. 'I stayed with you …'

Fizz sighed and turned around. He climbed the steps into his caravan. He was sad, not angry, just sad. At least it was over now.

Slowly everyone began to follow Fizz (not into his caravan, which would soon be very crowded, but into their own ones (and Dr Surprise walked Alice back to the cicrus (and then followed his short cut back, getting to bed much, much later than everyone else))).

The Ringmaster was finally left by himself.

His friends, those people who had been his circus family for many years, had turned their backs on him. They didn't *hate* him for what he had done. Of course they knew he hadn't done it to be mean, or spiteful, or wicked. They knew he was a human being, and had simply been weak and vain and afraid. But he needed to be more than that, better than that if they were ever to follow him again, if they were ever to hold him in the high estimation they had once held him, and that wasn't going to happen. Not easily. Not quickly.

'I'm sorry,' he said to the empty car park, before going back to bed.

The following day a circus-ish meeting was held, in the space between the caravans.

The Ringmaster's caravan had gone, vanished in the night, and in its place was left a bottom drawer with some money in it. It was his savings and he had left it for his old friends. (It wasn't a huge amount of money (not a prince's ransom, certainly), but it was a kind gesture.)

Percy Late had got in touch with as many of the old acts as he could and they'd learnt that most of them had found jobs with various circuses scattered all over the country, so there was no chance of getting the old circus back together.

Besides, the Big Top and most of the ropes and equipment had been sold off too. They couldn't be a circus, not even a tiny eleven-person circus without a Big Top.

(Fortunately Miss Tremble's horses had been sent away to visit a cousin of hers in the country, so she was able to call on their help, and Captain Fox-Dingle used some of the

Ringmaster's money to buy Kate back from Duck'n'Gooseland (who had been happy to sell her, not having many ducks or geese left).)

After all they had been through they wanted to stick together and so, with no other option obvious to them, they went to see Neil Coward.

The following night *Neil Coward's Famous Cicrus* put on the best show it had ever mounted.

Dr Surprise did some high-class hypnotising.

Miss Tremble rode round on beautiful white horses (refreshed and better than ever after their holiday in the country).

The Fumbling Gloriosus and Bongo

Bongoton did a small, but brilliant clown show (she dropped things and he looked surprised, again and again).

Emerald Sparkles threw knives at Kevin, as he spun on a rotating board.

Percy Late spun his plate with elegance, wit and charm. (Mr Crudge, Alice's dad, handed him the plate, with a sequined flourish, but left the spinning to the master.)

And Fizz, his dad and Alice did a three-person act of lifting quite heavy things up that was a real highlight. In all my years of watching circus shows I've never seen feats of triple-strength like it.

I particularly enjoyed the bit where they got a volunteer from the audience (that night there were almost two people in) and lifted them, twirled them and passed them back and forth between one another as the music fanfared and crescendoed around them.

The reason I particularly enjoyed that was because *I* was that volunteer.

I like to think Fizz picked me, out of all the possible audience members he could've pointed at, because I reminded him a bit of his old friend Wystan Barboozul (who was a bearded boy; me being similarly bearded), but whatever the reason, he hefted me above his head and his dad hefted me higher and Alice delivered me back to my seat.

Oh! It was a glorious night.

And so that was how I, just a humble writer, first met the remarkable Fizzlebert Stump and his friends and family.

Now, all these years later … now that Fizz is the Ringmaster of his own circus

(the second-youngest Ringmaster in circus history, apparently) ... he's asked me to write down some of his early adventures, because if things aren't written down, sooner or later the stories get forgotten.

I am honoured to have been given this job and have performed it to the utmost of my ability across these six volumes, without making anything up or embroidering the truth in the slightest.

But I get ahead of myself, talking about things that have nothing to do with the story I'm telling you.

Let's wrap things up.

Mrs Leavings escaped from police custody and fled to Acapulco and was last heard of working as a deckchair attendant, which is OK work if you like that sort of thing. (Fortunately she didn't.)

Mr Pinkbottle also escaped just before his case went to trial, but no one knows for certain where he ended up. But here are three rumours I've heard.

(1) He drowned in the great M6 custard spill of 2011.

(2) He changed his name to Siobhan, invented a time machine and introduced jazz music to fourteenth-century Paris.

Or (3) he moved back in with his mum and dad.

I don't know which, if any, of those is the truth.

What I do know is that, when he was arrested, Pinkbottle's Supermarket was taken over by the staff in a bloodless coup (I didn't often mention it, but of course there were other people working there besides our circus friends). They renamed it *A Good Shop For Food* and it remains a popular shopping destination for people in the area who like food.

So that's nice. A happy ending for them, able to get on with their jobs without a pig of a boss breathing down their necks and being unpleasant.

As far as I know the Ringmaster wasn't heard from again. Perhaps he shaved his moustache and joined another circus at the bottom, starting as a sawdust sweeper or minor juggler. Or perhaps he went and got an entirely different job, a change of direction. What is certain is that he never returned to

Aldonia and became king and lucky mascot of the nation of his birth, because it would've been in the newspapers, wouldn't it?

Mr and Mrs Stump offered to use the last of the Ringmaster's money to have the lettering on the side of Neil Coward's caravan repainted.

He refused to take the money. Secretly he'd grown fond of the word 'cicrus'.

Word got round about the new acts appearing in his ring and in the next town they visited audience numbers were in the low thirties, then in the high fifties and by the following spring there were nights when they almost sold out the Medium Top.

Neil Coward's Famous Cicrus wasn't such a bad place after all, it turned out, and even the acts who weren't very good when Fizz had joined, got better. That happens sometimes, just being in a place where good things are happening, where great acts are showbizzing around you … it's inspiring, it makes you work harder, it pulls your socks up.

One night, a few weeks into the cicrus's new life, Fizz woke in the night to hear a honking outside his caravan.

He unbuckled the straps, slipped his feet in his slippers and rummaged in one of the kitchen cupboards.

He knew the noise, recognised the voice. He'd not heard it for ages and he wanted to make sure he met it in the right way.

He stood up and made his way to the

caravan door, clutching a cold tin in his hand.

He hooked a finger into the ring on the top of the can and, with a pop, pulled back the lid.

The honking outside grew louder, more excited.

The smell of pilchards in tomato sauce filled the caravan.

Fizz opened the door and before he could step outside was knocked to the ground by the heavy, smelly, wonderful shape of a pilchard-seeking sea lion.

Fish had found his way home.

And so, it's not an unhappy ending.

Sure, Fizz wasn't in the brilliant circus he was in at the start of the book, but sometimes that's the way it goes: the place you end up is

different to where you begin. Sometimes Different is a Good Thing.

He and Alice and his dad lifted things up.

And he was happy.

And, well, to be absolutely honest, he couldn't really ask for more than that.

HAVE YOU READ GRETA ZARGO?

Greta Zargo needs a big scoop if she's going to win the Prilchard-Spritzer Medal, the quite famous award for great reporting. But big scoops are in short supply in her quiet little town, until a mysterious silver robot descends from the sky …

TURN OVER FOR A SNEAK PEEK

PROLOGUE

Earth

LAST SUNDAY

NO ONE ON Earth knew that their planet was being observed.

No one realised that vast computer brains waited, hidden in high Earth orbit, plotting and planning the planet's destruction.

No one detected the silvery robot as it descended from the blue summer's sky with a slow, quiet whoosh of unknown energy and flew towards the small English town of Middling Otherbridge.

No one knew that only three things stood in the way of their complete and utter annihilation: one elderly parrot, one eleven-year-old spelling mistake and one intrepid young newspaper-reporter-cum-schoolgirl in search of a Big Scoop.

And yet, that's exactly what's at stake in this book: *the fate of the entire planet Earth*.

Now read on …

CHAPTER ONE

Upper Lowerbridge, England, Earth

LAST MONDAY

WHEN GRETA ZARGO'S parents accidentally died she was left the family home, everything in it, a large bank account, a library card, three hamsters (now dead, stuffed and on the mantelpiece), a lifetime subscription to *Clipboarding Weekly* magazine (*the* magazine for all clipboarding enthusiasts) and a pair of scissors she was to never run with. Since she had only been a baby at the time, all of this was held in trust for her by her Aunt Tabitha until her eighth birthday.*

As soon as she turned eight Greta moved out of her aunt's house and into her own one, just over the road. Naturally her aunt kept an eye on Greta, whenever she remembered to, and in the three years that followed absolutely no disasters had occurred. Other than perhaps that one time the fire engine had to come to get her off the roof. But even then, as Greta pointed out in a stiffly worded letter to the school newspaper, she hadn't *actually* been stuck. So, no disasters at all.

It was in the bathroom of that very house that Greta Zargo was now hiding underneath the bubbles in a deep, hot bath she'd

**The relevant sentence in her parents' Last Will and Testament should, of course, have read 'eighteenth birthday' but contained a legally binding spelling mistake. (It should be noted that this is not the spelling mistake mentioned in the Prologue; that's a different one made around the same time.)*

run for herself. She soaked in the steaming tub, and breathed deep of the foamy perfume. This wasn't the best idea since it tickled her nose and made her sneeze, which blew a hole in the bubbles through which she could see the bathroom ceiling.

The ceiling, being a little grey at the edges, reminded her of her disappointing morning.

It was the summer and, being a girl of sparky determination, she'd got herself a holiday job as a Very Junior Reporter for *The Local Newspaper*.* It wasn't a real holiday job, since there are laws against employing eleven-year-old children, but when she'd followed Mr Inglebath (the newspaper's editor) across the park, through the library and into the swimming pool, asking to work for him, she had seemed so like a girl who

* *The Local Newspaper* was an award-winning newspaper, as it proudly boasted on the front cover. It had won the Most Accurately Titled Print Periodical Prize four years running, until the *Adverts for Old Fridges (Incorporating Gossip & Photos of Local People) Weekly* beat it to the top spot last time round.

wouldn't take no for an answer that he'd said yes.

He quickly explained, however, that he wasn't going to pay her (though she was welcome to a biscuit or two whenever she visited the office).

This was fine by Greta. She wasn't in it for the money.

She had bought herself a new reporter's notebook and her aunt had made her a press badge with a tiny tape recorder hidden inside it.

When you pressed the button labelled 'Press' on the press badge it recorded everything it heard, which meant she didn't need to use the reporter's notebook to take notes, unless the press badge had run out of batteries, which it sometimes did. So, with the press badge pinned to her jacket and the notebook in her bag, just in case, she was ready to go out and report the news.

Oh, she had been so excited, and then ...

The problem was that as a Very Junior Reporter it was her job to go where her editor sent her and to cover the stories he told her to cover. That was just the way of things, and this morning Mr Inglebath had sent her to talk to Hari Socket about his missing Battenberg cake (he'd bought it for his son's birthday and had taken it out of the wrapper and put it on a plate in the kitchen from where it had mysteriously vanished while he was watching *Stop! Look! Redecorate!* in the front room). It had taken Greta two minutes and twenty-three seconds of investigation for her to realise this was *a rubbish story*. This was not *front page material*, and never would be, not unless a whole lot more cakes went missing, and what was the likelihood of that happening?

Had Greta been asked to explain exactly why she needed a bigger story to make her happy, she could have pointed to three very important reasons.

Firstly, halfway through the summer term she'd been kicked off the school newspaper for having published those photographs of the Head kissing Mr Biggingstock in the stationery cupboard. Being told that she couldn't be a reporter any more made Greta more determined than ever to be a reporter (in the same way that, when as a very young girl Aunt Tabitha had once told her not to eat soap, she proceeded to demolish two whole bars before burping bubbles for the rest of the week). When school started up again in September, she'd write in her 'What I did during the holidays' story: *I became an Ace Reporter and got the Big Scoop.*

(The 'Big Scoop' being an impressive story no one else had discovered, rather than an oversized trowel or a standard portion of ice cream.)

Secondly, there was the clause in her parents' Last Will and Testament (clause seventeen) that said: *Darling, try to find out as much stuff as you can. Knowledge is fun and useful. The world needs bright, inquisitive people like you to help it get by. Darling, be brilliant.*

Ever since she'd read the Last Will, sat on her aunt's workbench as a little girl (burping bubbles), she'd tried to live up to it. She'd stuck her nose in all the mysteries she could find, and all the books and up all the trees, and that was simply the way it was.

And thirdly and finally, a simple, boring cake theft was not the sort of story that would win her the Prilchard-Spritzer Medal, the quite famous award for great journalism.

It was a beautiful medal and would look lovely displayed above the mantelpiece next to her swimming certificate and the Best in Show rosette her mother had won once with a particularly handsome terrapin. Just think how *that* would look when she got back to school: *Sacked School Reporter Scoops Sensational Reporter Prize*. That would show them doubly. Twice over. Extra! Extra! Read all about it!

Lying back in the bath with great mountains of foam drifting around her, Greta shut her eyes, dozed and dreamt of the day Mr Prilchard* himself would loop the medal's ribbon around her neck. The wavering floral scent of the bubble bath hid the smell of fish that always followed Mr Prilchard around (even an imaginary Mr Prilchard in

* *Mr Prilchard owned Prilchard's Pilchards (and Other Fish), the fishmonger's who sponsored the prize.*

a daydream) and Greta smiled broadly.

As she began her acceptance speech a bell rang.

That's odd, she thought.

As she began her short list of *thank you*s and longer list of *I told you so*s again, the bell rang a second time.

She woke up in the bath realising that it was actually the doorbell ringing.

Grabbing a towel, she stepped on to the toilet, pushed open the fanlight at the top of the bathroom window and peered out.

There was no one there.

'That's odd,' she said to herself.

She had heard, just before she reached the window, a slow quiet whoosh of unknown energy and, assuming it was the asthmatic blackbird* that liked to hang out in the big oak tree across the road, she ignored it.

* *The slow quiet whoosh of unknown energy had actually been a silvery robot floating above her doorstep, which flew off as she opened the window.*

Getting back in the bath, she found her daydream rather spoilt. The assembled crowd had mostly gone home and it seemed silly reading her acceptance speech to the few who remained, since they were mostly just there for the free buffet.

She got out of the bath and made herself some toast instead.

CHAPTER TWO

Cestrypip

965 LIGHT YEARS FROM EARTH
107,242 YEARS AGO

THE PEOPLE OF the planet Cestrypip had a unique life cycle: like insects on Earth they went through a series of stages.

After a five year period as a large, wriggling white grub, and a further fifty or sixty years as a green-skinned, lizardish humanoid doing all the usual stuff humanoids do (having jobs, arguing about sports and giving birth to large, white maggoty grubs) the Cestrypippians would give away all their possessions, say farewell to their families and put down roots, put out leaves and spend a century as a slow-dreaming tree. When the dream was ended, they would shed their bark, pull their feet from the soil and spend a vigorous decade in their final life stage as a shouty but encouraging PE teacher.

DISCOVER ALL FIZZLEBERT STUMP'S ADVENTURES